magical bedtime stories

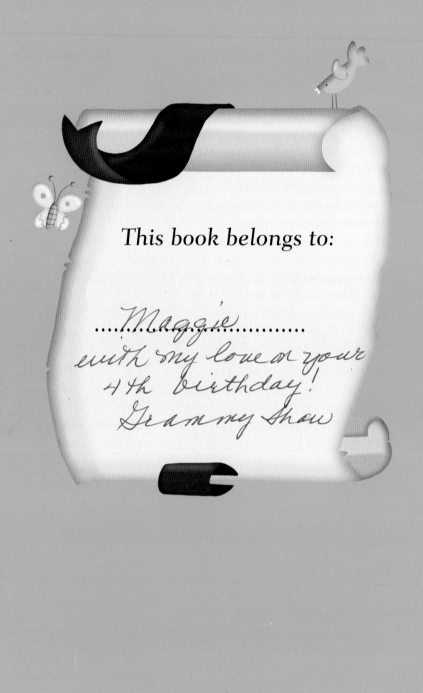

This book belongs to:

......Maggie............

with my love on your
4th birthday!
Grammy Shaw

magical bedtime stories

Illustrated by
Jo Parry &
Marie Allen

ARCTURUS

ARCTURUS

This edition published in 2015 by Arcturus Publishing Limited
26/27 Bickels Yard, 151–153 Bermondsey Street,
London SE1 3HA

Written and designed by Nicola Baxter
Illustrated by Jo Parry and Marie Allen
Edited by Kate Overy and Frances Evans

ISBN: 978-1-78404-894-5
CH004724NT
Supplier 26, Date 0815, Print run 4218

Printed in China

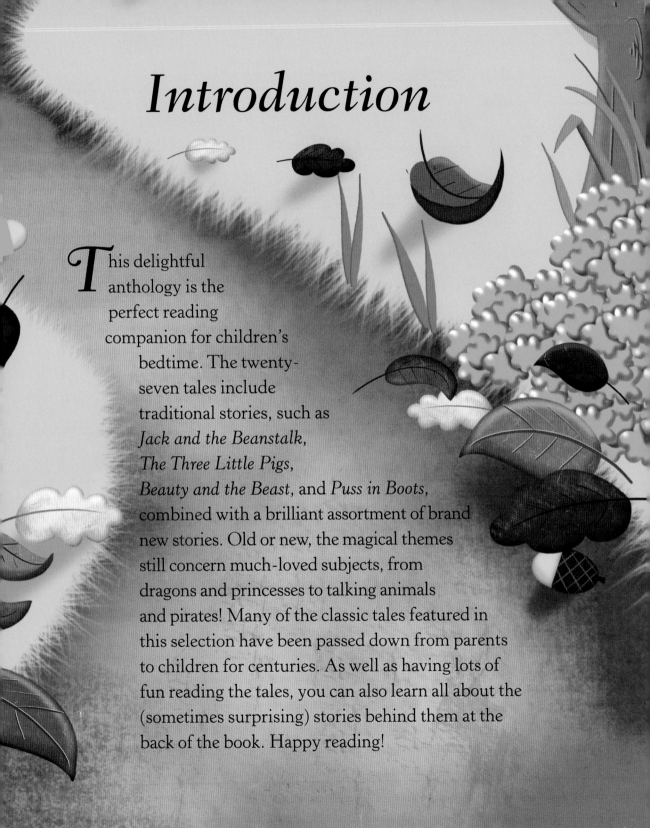

Introduction

*T*his delightful
anthology is the
perfect reading
companion for children's
bedtime. The twenty-
seven tales include
traditional stories, such as
Jack and the Beanstalk,
The Three Little Pigs,
Beauty and the Beast, and *Puss in Boots*,
combined with a brilliant assortment of brand
new stories. Old or new, the magical themes
still concern much-loved subjects, from
dragons and princesses to talking animals
and pirates! Many of the classic tales featured in
this selection have been passed down from parents
to children for centuries. As well as having lots of
fun reading the tales, you can also learn all about the
(sometimes surprising) stories behind them at the
back of the book. Happy reading!

Contents

Jack and the Beanstalk

A long time ago, a boy named Jack lived with his mother. They were very poor.

"We will have to sell the cow, Jack," said his mother one day. "Take her to market and get as much for her as you can."

Jack set off along the road with the cow. He wished he did not have to walk all the way to market.

Before he had gone very far, Jack met an old man.

"I can see you are a clever boy," he told Jack, "so listen to me.
If you give me your cow, I will give you something much
more precious."

"All right," said Jack, without thinking very hard.
The old man handed over a small bag.

"In there," he said, "are five magic beans.
They are very rare indeed."

Jack couldn't wait to get
home with his bargain.

"You did *WHAT*?" yelled his mother when Jack showed her the beans. "You silly boy. There's no such thing as a magic bean."

Angrily, she threw the beans out of the window and sent Jack to bed without dinner.

When Jack woke up the next morning, the room was dark. A huge beanstalk was growing just outside and blocking the window. It had grown from the magic beans!

Jack didn't stop to think about what had happened. He saw that the beanstalk had many, many thick branches, and he was a boy who loved to climb. In a second, he had crawled out of the window and was climbing up the beanstalk as fast as he could.

Jack climbed and climbed. The beanstalk grew up through the clouds. At the top, Jack was amazed to find that he was in another country. Everything seemed very big there. Jack would have wondered about that if he had not been worrying about something much more important.

He had not had dinner last night and now he had missed breakfast. His belly was rumbling!

Far away across some fields, Jack could see a huge castle. There was sure to be some food there, he thought. He set off toward it.

The castle door was enormous, but Jack knocked boldly. A woman opened it.

"Quick! Quick! Come in!" she cried. "If my husband the giant comes home, he'll eat you!"

Jack hurried inside. A moment later he heard a great roar:

Fee-fi-fo-fum, I smell the blood of an Englishman.
Be he alive or be he dead,
I'll grind his bones to make my bread!

"Quick!" cried the woman, and she pushed Jack into the oven to hide. Luckily, it was not hot!

Peering out, Jack saw the
giant eating his dinner.
When the giant had finished,
he began to count gold coins
into little bags. At last,
he fell asleep.

Quick as a flash, Jack
dashed out of the oven,
grabbed a bag of coins,
and scampered down
the beanstalk.

Jack's mother was overjoyed to see the coins. For a few months, all was well, but then the money began to run out. Jack decided to climb the beanstalk again. He headed straight for the castle, where the kind woman opened the door. Just as before, a few moments later the ground began to shake and a voice could be heard roaring:

Fee-fi-fo-fum, I smell the blood of an Englishman.
Be he alive or be he dead,
I'll grind his bones to make my bread!

"Oh no, not again!" cried the woman. "Quick! Hide!"

This time, when the giant had eaten, he asked for his
magic hen. To Jack's amazement, the hen laid a golden egg!
The giant smiled and went to sleep.

Once more, Jack made his escape. Instead of stealing the
golden egg, he picked up the hen and ran home as fast
as he could.

With a hen that laid a golden egg each day, Jack and his mother had nothing more to worry about. Even so, Jack decided to have one last adventure.

Everything happened just as before, but when the giant had eaten, he called, "Bring me my harp!"

His wife brought a golden harp, which began to play all by itself. At once, the giant fell asleep. Jack grabbed the harp and ran to the door.

"*STOP!*" cried the magic harp. The giant awoke at once and stormed after Jack. When Jack reached the beanstalk, he hurled himself down it.

"Mother!" he yelled. "Quick! We need to chop down the beanstalk!"

Jack worked hard and soon the huge beanstalk came crashing to the ground. The giant tumbled with it, never to trouble anyone again. Jack could not climb to magic lands now, but he and his mother lived happily ever after.

Chicken Little

*T*here was once a small chick called Chicken Little.
One day, as he was scratching about under an old oak
tree, an acorn fell on his head. Chicken Little didn't see
the acorn. *"Ouch!"* he cried. "The sky is falling down! I must go
and tell the King."

Chicken Little ran through the farmyard,
where he met Henny Penny.

"Oh, Henny Penny," cried Chicken Little,
"the sky is falling down and I'm going
to tell the King."

"*Cluck! Cluck!* I will come too," said Henny Penny.

Chicken Little and Henny Penny were just going through the farmyard gate when they met Cocky Locky.

"Oh, Cocky Locky," cried Chicken Little, "the sky is falling down and we're going to tell the King."

"*Doodle-doo!* I will come too," said Cocky Locky.

Chicken Little, Henny Penny, and Cocky Locky were
hurrying past the pond when they met Ducky Lucky.

"Oh, Ducky Lucky," cried Chicken Little,
"the sky is falling down and we're going
to tell the King."

"*Quack! Quack!* I will come too,"
said Ducky Lucky.

Chicken Little, Henny Penny,
Cocky Locky, and Ducky Lucky
were scurrying along the lane when
they met Goosey Loosey.

"Oh, Goosey Loosey," cried
Chicken Little, "the sky is
falling down and we're going
to tell the King."

"*Honk! Honk!* I will come too,"
said Goosey Loosey.

Chicken Little, Henny Penny,
Cocky Locky, Ducky Lucky, and
Goosey Loosey were turning the
corner when they met Turkey Lurkey.

"Oh, Turkey Lurkey," cried
Chicken Little, "the sky is
falling down and we're going
to tell the King."

"*Gobble! Gobble!* I will come too,"
said Turkey Lurkey.

Chicken Little, Henny Penny, Cocky Locky, Ducky Lucky, Goosey Loosey, and Turkey Lurkey had come to the edge of the wood when they met Foxy Loxy.

"My, my," said Foxy Loxy, "where are you all off to on this fine day?"

"Oh, Foxy Loxy," cried Chicken Little, "the sky is falling down and we're going to tell the King."

"Then come with me," said Foxy Loxy. "I will take you to the King."

So Chicken Little, Henny Penny, Cocky Locky, Ducky Lucky, Goosey Loosey, and Turkey Lurkey followed Foxy Loxy. He took them into the wood, where his family was waiting for dinner.

Poor Chicken Little, Henny Penny, Cocky Locky, Ducky Lucky, Goosey Loosey, and Turkey Lurkey were never seen again.

And the fox family lived happily ever after, although ever so many acorns fell on their heads.

The Very Secret Treasure

A legend tells that long ago and far away there was a castle. In the castle, there was a secret room. In the room, there was a secret chest. In the chest, there was a key. It was the key to a very secret treasure.

There was once a King who had one son. On his eighteenth birthday, Prince Fillipo was summoned by his father.

"The time has come," said the King, "for you to go on a quest. You know the legend of the secret key to the very secret treasure. All you have to do is find the key and claim the treasure."

"That's hardly a challenge, Father," replied the Prince.

Prince Filippo called Jago, his page, and told him to start packing. Within the hour, the Prince left the palace on his finest steed. Jago, on a heftier horse, was carrying all the princely baggage.

"First," said the Prince, "we must find the castle. I have a picture of it here. We will go toward the mountains."

"Sire," said Jago quietly, "in the picture, it is by the sea."

"That's exactly what I meant," replied the Prince.

A few weeks later, the Prince and his page looked down from a clifftop and saw the castle. They were soon riding up to the gates. As there was no one to be seen, the Prince got off his horse and entered the castle.

"This is the secret room," he declared.

"But, Sire," said Jago, "it's not very secret."

"Er … that was a joke," replied the Prince. "Follow me!"

The two searched the castle. Just as the Prince was about to give up, Jago spotted a hidden handle. He touched it, and at once the wall slid back, revealing a secret room!

"I've found it!" exclaimed the Prince, flopping down. "But there is no chest here!"

"Sire, I think you're sitting on it," suggested Jago.

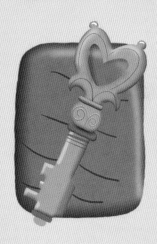

The Prince flung open the chest.
Inside, glinting gently, was the
famous key.

"I will find the lock that this key
opens," cried the Prince. "Soon I'll
be even richer and more famous than
I am now."

As they crossed the courtyard, the
Prince and his page were amazed to see a
beautiful girl sitting near a well.

"I see you have found the key,"
she said. "You are very close
to the treasure now."

"I know," said the Prince. "Please
don't delay me in my quest. I need
to search the castle."

But the key did not fit any lock in the castle.

"What a waste of time this has been," the Prince complained.

Jago looked shyly at the girl. "I believe I know the secret of the key," he said, blushing. "Could it be the key to your heart?"

"I am Princess Elena," smiled the girl. "Only a brave, clever, and kind person could complete this quest, and you have done it. The secret treasure is my hand in marriage. You have won the right to become my husband and rule my kingdom with me … if you wish to."

"Well, I was expecting gold," sighed the Prince, "but if you insist …"

"I wasn't talking to *you*," said the Princess firmly.

Filippo glanced from the Princess to his page and back again. They both looked ridiculously happy.

"I don't believe it!" spluttered the Prince.

Jago said goodbye to his master and set off to live happily
ever after. The Prince made his lonely way home.
The journey gave him time to think.

When he returned,
he went straight to the King.

"I have failed, Father," he said.
"I was not clever enough or
kind enough to win this quest."

The King smiled. "But you have
learned a great deal, my boy,"
he said, "and come back a better man.
That is what a quest is for, and it is
the best treasure of all."

Puss in Boots

Once there was a miller who had three sons. When he died, he left the mill to his eldest son and his donkey to his second son. The third son was not so lucky. All that was left as his share was the family cat.

"I'm sorry, Puss," said the miller's son. "I don't know what we are going to do. How can I even look after you with no job and no money?"

"Don't worry," said the cat. "Just give me some boots and a bag and we'll be fine."

The miller's son was puzzled, but he did as
the cat asked. Puss pulled on the boots and filled
the bag with lettuce leaves. Then he marched
off to a meadow, put down the bag, and sat
down to wait.

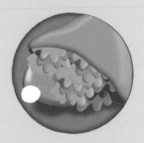

Just as Puss had planned, before long a little rabbit hopped over to the bag and began to nibble at the lettuce. In a flash, Puss scooped up the bag. Holding it carefully so that the rabbit could not escape, he hurried off to the King's palace.

When he saw the King, Puss swept off his hat and bowed low.

"Your Majesty," he said, "may I present you with this very fine rabbit, a gift from my master, the Marquis of Carrabas?"

The king frowned. "I don't believe I know him," he said, "but you deserve a treat from the palace kitchens."

While he was tucking into a tasty treat, Puss overheard the servants talking. The very next day, the King and his daughter would be taking a drive by the river.

Puss returned to his master. In the morning, he told him, "Go for a swim in the river. If anyone asks, say that your name is the Marquis of Carrabas."

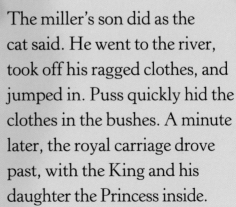

The miller's son did as the cat said. He went to the river, took off his ragged clothes, and jumped in. Puss quickly hid the clothes in the bushes. A minute later, the royal carriage drove past, with the King and his daughter the Princess inside.

"Stop the carriage!" cried the King. "Why, it is the clever cat who came to see me yesterday."

Puss heaved a great sigh. "I wish, your Majesty, I could present my master, the Marquis of Carrabas, to you today, but something dreadful has happened. While he was swimming in the river, a thief stole all his clothes!"

"Oh no!" cried the King and the Princess.

At once, the King asked for a suit of fine clothes to be brought from the palace. The miller's son got dressed behind the bushes and shyly came forward. He looked very handsome.

"My dear Marquis," beamed the King, "may I present my daughter, the Princess? Do come and ride with us."

Meanwhile, Puss was scampering on ahead. He saw a
man making hay in a meadow. "The King will be here in
a moment," Puss told him. "My master, the Marquis of
Carrabas, will be very grateful if you tell the King that he
owns all the land around here."

"I can do that," said the man, "but let's hope the ogre who
lives in that castle doesn't hear me. The land is his."

"What a fine hay meadow!" cried the King, when he came
along a few minutes later. "Tell me, my man, whose is it?"

"It belongs to the Marquis of Carrabas, your Majesty,"
the man replied.

While this was happening, Puss had hurried to the ogre's castle. When the huge ogre opened the door, Puss spoke up boldly. "I have heard," he said, "that you are a great magician. Is that true?"

"Come in," replied the ogre, "and I will show you!"

In a flash, the ogre turned himself into a fierce lion.

Puss jumped up onto the furniture.

"Well," he said, "I'm sure it's easy for a big, strong ogre to become a big, strong lion. But could you become a tiny, weak mouse?"

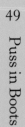

"Just watch me!" roared the ogre. At once, he became
a tiny mouse, scampering across the room.

Puss pounced! He munched up the mouse and looked around.
"This castle is the perfect home for my master,
the Marquis of Carrabas," he said.

When the King saw the castle, he was very impressed.
"The Marquis is just the kind of young man
I should like my daughter to marry,"
he said. The Princess agreed!

So Puss, the Princess, and
the miller's son lived
happily ever after.

Up, Up, and Away!

*T*here was once a family of rabbits who lived in a meadow. They were Father Rabbit, Mother Rabbit, and six little rabbits called:

Ashley, Bella, Chloe, Daniel, Emily … and Fred. Fred was the smallest, but he tried very hard to do everything his brothers and sisters did.

One morning, the little rabbits went out into the meadow for some hopping and jumping practice.

"I can hop higher than any of you!" cried Ashley. He jumped over a toadstool, a very surprised cow, and the little stream that ran through the meadow.

"We can do that!" chorused the other little rabbits.
One by one, they followed their brother. *Hop, hop, hop!*
Last came Fred. He jumped over the toadstool with ease.
Hop! He cleared the cow by a whisker. Hop! He ran to
the bank of the stream and sprang into the air. *Splash!*

"Poor little Fred," his brothers and sisters laughed.
"You'll never be able to jump as far as us!"

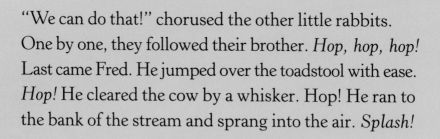

Father Rabbit found Fred drying
his ears in the sunshine.

"Don't worry, son," he said.
"All you need is practice.
Just hop and jump
whenever you get
the chance."

Fred nodded. From
that moment,
whenever he saw
something to jump
over, he jumped.
Little by little,
his hopping and
jumping improved.

He went out into the meadow in search of new things to jump over. He saw a patch of flowers. *Hop!*

He saw a piece of rope stretched across the meadow. *Hoppety-hop!*

He saw a fence he had never noticed before. *Hoppety-hop-HOP!*

Fred landed with a bump and found that he wasn't on the other side of a fence. He was inside a huge basket! As he stretched on his tiptoes to look over the side, he felt the basket begin to move.

Fred couldn't believe his eyes. He was in the basket of a hot air balloon, and his brothers and sisters were far below. As the men in charge of the balloon seized the rope and began to pull the basket safely down to the ground, the little rabbits below began to clap and wave.

"Well done, Fred! You've jumped higher than any of us!" they cheered.

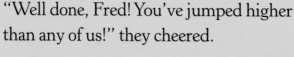

The Gingerbread Man

Long ago, there lived a little old man and a little old woman in a little old cottage in the country.

One day, the little old man went to work in the garden, and the little old woman baked some cookies. When she had finished, she had some dough left over, so she made it into a gingerbread man and put him in the oven.

Soon a delicious smell filled the kitchen. The little old woman took the gingerbread man out of the oven and put him on one side to cool. Then she made some decorations. She gave him a black tie, two shiny eyes, three brown buttons, red hands and feet, and a big smile!

The little old woman opened the door to call her husband. Suddenly, the gingerbread man jumped down onto the floor and ran out of the door!

"Stop!" cried the little old woman. But the gingerbread man just laughed and began to sing a little song, "Run, run, as fast as you can! You can't catch me, I'm the gingerbread man!"

He ran past the little old man, through the gate and off down the road. The little old man shouted, "Hey! Come back!"

But the gingerbread man ran on. "Run, run, as fast as you can! You can't catch me, I'm the gingerbread man!" he sang, as the little old woman and the little old man ran after him.

Before long, the gingerbread man passed a cow in a field.

"Yoooou look tasty," mooed the cow. She set off after the gingerbread man, the little old woman, and the little old man.

The gingerbread man just laughed. "Run, run, as fast as you can!" he sang. "You can't catch me, I'm the gingerbread man!"

A horse heard the song and raised her head.

"I saaaaaay," she neighed, "you look good to eat!" She galloped off down the road after the gingerbread man, the little old woman, the little old man, and the cow.

"Ha ha!" sang the gingerbread man. "Run, run, as fast as you can! You can't catch me, I'm the gingerbread man!"

A rooster saw the gingerbread man run past.

"I love cookies," he crowed. "Yes, I cock-a-doodle-doooo!"

He flapped off after the gingerbread man, the little old woman, the little old man, the cow, and the horse.

"Ho, ho!" chortled the gingerbread man. "Run, run, as fast as you can! You can't catch me, I'm the gingerbread man!"

"Oink! Oink!" snuffled a hungry pig. "I smell dinner!" He set off, as fast as his little pink trotters would carry him, after the gingerbread man, the little old woman, the little old man, the cow, the horse, and the rooster.

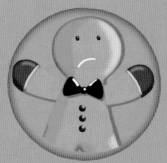

The gingerbread man ran on and on, until he came to a river. He didn't know how to swim and the river was too wide to jump over.

He looked around. The little old woman, the little old man, the cow, the horse, the rooster, and the pig were getting nearer and nearer.

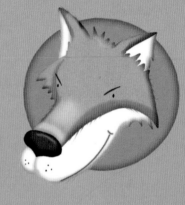

"Can I help at all?" asked a soft voice. Sitting on the bank was a big, red fox. "Why don't you jump on my back?" he said. "I'll carry you across."

The gingerbread man jumped on at once.
He didn't want to be eaten by the little
old woman, the little old man, the cow,
the horse, the rooster, or the pig. The fox
slid into the water.

"My toes!" cried the gingerbread man,
feeling a tiny splash.

"Climb onto my head," said the fox.
"You'll be safe there."

Now they were in the middle of the river, where the water was deeper. It almost reached the gingerbread man's feet.

"We're nearly there," said the fox. "Just perch on my nose."

So the gingerbread man climbed onto the fox's nose, but as soon as he did so, the fox tossed him up into the air! The gingerbread man flew up, up, up and then down, down, down … right into the fox's open mouth!

When the little old woman, the little old man, the cow, the horse, the rooster, and the pig reached the river, the fox was already on the other side. He was licking his lips.

And there was no sign at all of the gingerbread man.

The Dragon and the Princess

Once upon a time, in a country far away, there lived a dragon. He was not a very bad dragon, as dragons go, but most people kept well away from his cave in the Misty Mountains. His name was Magnus.

Like most dragons, Magnus was really only interested in one thing – treasure. His cave was dripping with jewels, and piles of gold and silver covered the floor. Magnus knew exactly how much treasure he had. He was perfectly happy.

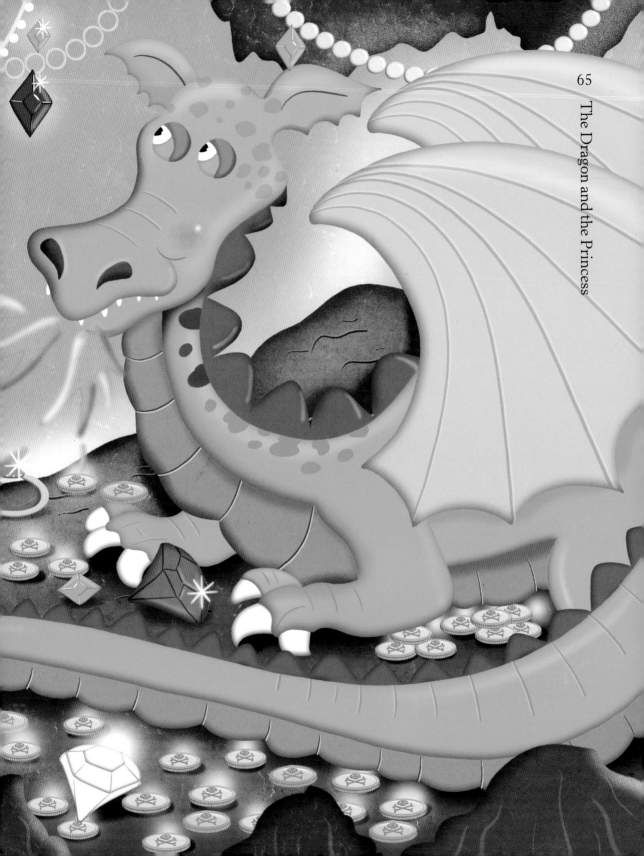

One day in spring, Magnus came out of his cave to stretch his wings. He flew around the mountain peaks and enjoyed himself trying out some dragon acrobatics.

He was just finishing a wobbly loop-the-loop when he noticed something. Far below, a procession of people and animals was slowly making its way along a narrow mountain path, led by a girl wearing a crown and riding a white horse.

As soon as he saw the group, Magnus began to wonder if they might be carrying gold and jewels. The glint of the girl's crown caught his eye. Here was a chance to add to his treasure store.

With what he hoped was a terrifying roar, Magnus flew down and landed just in front of the visitors. He saw at once that the girl in front was wearing royal robes and was probably a Princess. Her first words showed he was right.

"I am Princess Merlina!" she said. "And you are in my way!"

Magnus frowned. No one talks to a dragon like that! He took a deep breath and blew scary flames from his nostrils.

The Princess didn't seem frightened, but her horse reared up. Although the Princess clung on, her crown slipped off her head, rolled over the edge of the path, and down into the deep valley below, twinkling as it fell.

Magnus couldn't help it. He forgot about trying to frighten the Princess and peered down to see where the sparkly treasure had fallen. Merlina scrambled from her horse.

The Princess and the dragon had exactly the same thought at exactly the same moment: *I must get that crown!*

All Magnus had to do was swoop down, seize the crown, and fly away with it. The Princess interrupted his thoughts. "Thank goodness!" she cried. "That's only my travel crown. My two most precious crowns are in my jewel chest. Please, please, take that crown if you must, but don't take my jewel chest!"

Magnus spread his wings and snorted a few more flames to show he meant business. The Princess sighed and beckoned two servants. They staggered forward, each holding one handle of a huge chest.

Completely forgetting about the crown below, Magnus seized the chest with the claws of his scaly feet. Only the thought of the gold and jewels inside gave him the strength to lift it, and it was not until sunset that he reached his cave.

Meanwhile, the Princess sent her page boy to clamber down and rescue her crown, and the royal party left the Misty Mountains with all possible speed.

That night, Magnus snapped the lock of the chest and opened it to find … a picnic! For a moment, he was furious that the Princess has tricked him, but not for long. It was a royal picnic after all, and even jewels don't stop a dragon's tummy from rumbling!

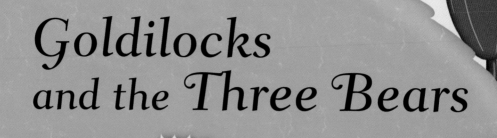

Goldilocks
and the Three Bears

Once upon a time, there was a family of bears who lived in a cottage in a forest. Father Bear had a deep, growly voice, Mother Bear had a warm, soft voice, and Baby Bear had a high, squeaky voice.

One morning, before breakfast, the bears went out for a walk.

A few minutes later, a little girl came along. When she saw that the cottage door was not quite closed, she did something very naughty. She marched up the front path, pushed open the door, and went inside!

The little girl's name was Goldilocks, because she had bright yellow hair. After her walk in the woods, Goldilocks was hungry, so she looked around for something to eat.

On the kitchen table, she spotted three bowls of porridge. She went straight to the biggest bowl, picked up Father Bear's large spoon, and took a mouthful.

"Ouch!" cried Goldilocks. "Much too hot!"

She picked up Mother Bear's medium-sized spoon and tasted *her* porridge.

"*Eeeeeuuuuw!* Much too sweet!" she said.

Last of all, she tried Baby Bear's porridge.
Now Goldilocks didn't say a word.
It was just right, so she was much too busy eating!

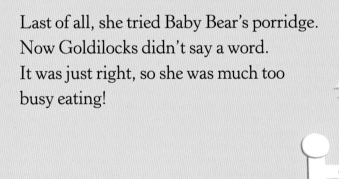

When she was full, Goldilocks wandered into the living room. She looked around for a comfy chair. She saw three chairs – one large, one medium-sized, and one tiny.

Goldilocks climbed onto the huge armchair in the corner. Ow! It was much too hard.

She leapt down and went over to the middle-sized chair.
Goldilocks hauled herself up and nearly disappeared!
The chair was so soft, she almost sank
beneath the cushions.

Goldilocks scrambled out and headed for the smallest chair of all. It looked perfect. She sat down on it...

CRAAAAACK!

BUMP!

OUCH!

Suddenly, Goldilocks felt very tired. She spotted some stairs in the corner of the room and went over to them.

At the top of the stairs was a bedroom with three beds.
Goldilocks tested the largest bed.

"Ouch! Too hard again!" she cried.

She jumped onto the middle-sized bed.

"Ooof! Too soft!" she groaned.

The smallest bed stood under the window.
Goldilocks lay down. Aaah! Perfect!
In a second, she was fast asleep.

While Goldilocks slept upstairs, the three bears came back from their walk. Immediately, Father Bear saw that something was wrong.

"Someone's been eating my porridge!" he growled.

"And someone's been eating my porridge!" said Mother Bear.

"And someone's been eating my porridge," cried Baby Bear, "and they've eaten it all up!"

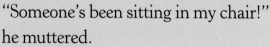

Father Bear strode into the living room.

"Someone's been sitting in my chair!" he muttered.

"Someone's been sitting in my chair, too," said Mother Bear.

"Oooh!" wailed Baby Bear. "Someone's been sitting in my chair – and it's broken!"

From upstairs there came a tiny snoring sound. The bears crept up the stairs and into the bedroom.

"Someone's been lying on my bed," said Father Bear.

"And someone's been lying on my bed," said Mother Bear.

"And someone's been lying on my bed," squeaked Baby Bear, "and she's still there!"

Just then, Goldilocks woke up and saw the three bears. She gave a little scream, climbed quickly out of the window, and ran home as fast as she could. The bears never saw her again.

The Other Frog Prince

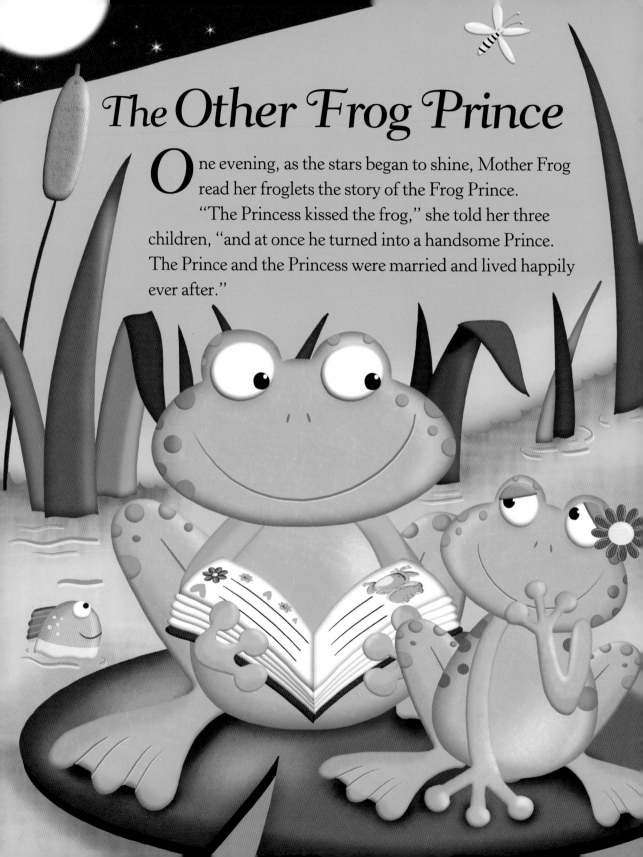

One evening, as the stars began to shine, Mother Frog read her froglets the story of the Frog Prince.

"The Princess kissed the frog," she told her three children, "and at once he turned into a handsome Prince. The Prince and the Princess were married and lived happily ever after."

Young Fiona Frog sighed contentedly and went to sleep.
Little Freddie Frog giggled and settled down on his lily pad.
But Felix Frog was too excited to sleep. There and then, he
decided he would find a beautiful Princess,
turn into a handsome Prince, and marry her.

As soon as he was old enough, Felix set out to make his dream come true. He said goodbye to his mother, his sister, and his brother and set off to find his Princess.
He hopped across fields…

paddled through puddles…

and swam across rivers…

... until one day, in the distance, he saw a magnificent castle. It had towers and turrets. Its flags and banners were covered with flowers, and its walls were pink.

"That," said Felix to himself, "is certainly the home of a beautiful Princess."

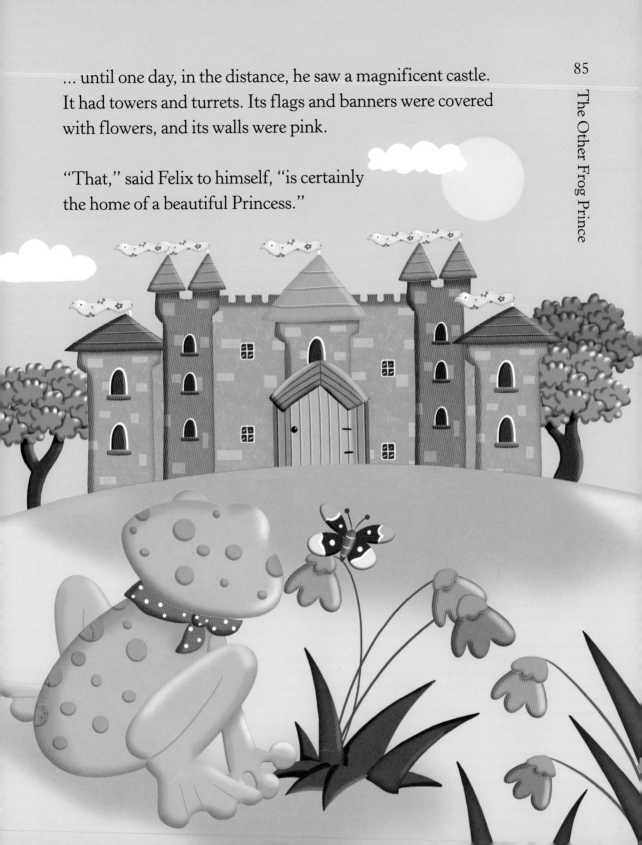

When he reached the castle, Felix found it was surrounded by wonderful gardens, and there, sitting under a flowering tree, was a Princess. She was certainly beautiful, but she looked bored and unhappy.

"She looks sad because she hasn't met me yet," said Felix to himself. He knew it might be difficult to persuade the Princess that he was really a Prince in disguise, so he hopped into a flowerbed and made himself a little crown from a golden flower.

Felix approached the Princess. He saw that she was holding a small picture of a young man. From time to time, she leaned down and kissed it with tears in her eyes.

Now Felix knew what to do. Instead of persuading the Princess to kiss him, he simply hopped onto the picture and waited. Sure enough, the Princess sighed, puckered up her lips, and leaned over.

"Eeeeeuuuurgh!" She flung the picture from her.
"Help! Eeeeeeuuuurgh! A nasty frog is on my picture of Prince Goodheart!"* she shrieked.

Just then, the young man in the picture hurtled through a nearby hedge and swept the Princess up into his arms.

"I will save you, my beloved!" he cried. "Forgive me for taking so long to return. I had trouble with my carriage."

While the Princess kissed her Prince, Felix hopped hurriedly away. His dreams were shattered. When he saw a pool of cool, shimmering water before him, he dived in with relief. He began to feel more like himself again.

A silvery voice interrupted him. "You've lost your crown, your Highness," said a charming young girl-frog, who was sitting on a lily leaf. She was holding his flower crown and wearing something similar herself.

"I'm … I'm not a Prince," stammered Felix, "not really."

"I'm not a Princess," smiled the new frog kindly, "but it's nice to pretend, isn't it?"

Felix had never been good with words. He thought of himself as more of an action frog. But at that moment, the pretty girl-frog's sparkling eyes inspired him to say, "You're certainly pretty enough to be a Princess!"

The end of this story is easy to tell. The Frog Princess kissed Felix and at once he became the handsome frog of her dreams. The Frog Princess and her Frog Prince were married and lived happily ever after.

Tom Thumb

Long ago there lived a woodsman and his wife who had no children. "If only we had a child to help me in the forest and be company for you in the house," said the woodsman sadly.

"If we had a child of our own," replied his wife, "I wouldn't mind if he or she was only as big as your thumb."

A few years later, their dreams came true, and they had a tiny baby. He really *was* tiny. His mother and father fed him the best food they could buy, but he never grew any bigger than his father's thumb. They named him Thomas, but his nickname soon became Tom Thumb.

Young Tom Thumb was a lively boy. He was full of plans and schemes, and his tiny body never seemed to stop him.

One day, he overheard his parents talking. "I'm not as young as I was," his father said. "It's getting harder to work in the forest on my own. It's a pity that young Tom can't help me."

Tom thought about this. He was upset that his parents didn't think he would be able to look after them as they got older.

The next day, when his father had set off into the forest, Tom jumped up on to the table where his mother was making bread and said, "I'm going to help Dad today. *Please harness up the horse so that I can drive the cart and take logs into town for him."

"Don't be silly, dear," said his mother, "and mind you don't fall in that flour! The horse is big and strong. You would never manage to control her."

"Please, Mother," Tom pleaded.

His mother was doubtful, but she knew
that Tom was a clever lad, so she did
as he asked. When the horse was
harnessed, however, she frowned.
"It's too dangerous," she said.
"I can't let you do this."

Tom smiled. "I'm not going to use the reins," he explained.
"Put me in the horse's ear. I'll tell her what to do instead."

Tom's mother placed him carefully in the horse's
warm ear. "Come on, old Beauty," he whispered.
"We're going into the forest.
You know the way. I'll tell
you when to stop."

To his mother's
amazement, the
horse trotted off.

As Tom went along, he passed two men on the road.
They owned a circus. "Did you see that?" one man said to
the other. "A horse and cart with no driver!"

"Let's follow it," said his friend. "We could use a clever
horse in our show."

The men crept closer. It was then that they saw the tiny boy
whispering in the horse's ear. That was even better! People
would pay a fortune to see a tiny boy like Tom Thumb!

Tom's father was amazed to see the horse and cart, but before he could speak, the two men hurried forward.

"What a fine boy you have," they said. "We will give you fifty gold pieces if you will let him come with us."

"Never!" cried the woodsman, but Tom whispered in his ear. "They are tricksters. Let's trick them! Take the money and I will escape from them later and come home."

That's exactly what happened. Tom's father took the money, and the two men took Tom, but that evening, Tom escaped into some long grass and the men could not find him anywhere. Then Tom hid in a cart that was going back toward his home and strolled in right on time for dinner!

How happy Tom's parents were to see their boy! Ever afterwards, *little* Tom was always known as a very *big* help to his family.

Princess Lola

The park at the weekend was full of dogs. There were big ones and little ones, smooth ones and hairy ones, well behaved ones and little scamps.

From the window of a very grand house, overlooking the park, Princess Lola watched them and wished she could join in.

Princess Lola had a special princess bed to sleep in. She had her own chef to prepare her meals. She even had jewels of her own. But she could not run in the park. Her owner was a real princess, and she did not have much time to play with Princess Lola.

One fine day, as Princess Lola looked longingly out of the window, she noticed it was open a tiny bit at the bottom. With a push of her paw and a nudge of her nose, she opened it just enough to slip out.

Princess Lola landed with a thud in a flowerbed, where a small, scruffy dog was digging.

"Woof! You scared me!" said the small, scruffy dog. "My name's Digger. What's yours?"

Digger laughed when he heard. "That's a
bit of a mouthful!" he said. "I'll just call
you Lola. Let's have a game of chase, then
I'll show you where to find some food."

Lola loved chasing across the park with the
breeze in her fur.

"I'm never going home," she said to herself.
Digger led her to the back of a restaurant.
"The chefs throw out all sorts of good stuff to
eat," he said

"Old food?" said Lola faintly. "Oh, actually,
I'm not feeling very hungry."

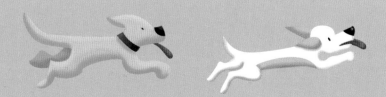

Next, Digger showed her a step in front of a huge house. "There's a warm place here," he said, "where we can sleep."

Princess Lola thought of her princess bed and shook her head. "I'm afraid I have to go," she said.

That night, when her owner came home, Princess Lola slipped into the house beside her. "Lola!" cried the Princess, "I've missed you all day. I tell you what, why don't we go for a walk in the park tomorrow, just us two?" Princess Lola barked in agreement. Although she liked her comfy bed and nice food, she loved spending time with her owner most of all. And she was looking forward to another run in the park with Digger.

The Magic Porridge Pot

Once upon a time, there was a little girl who lived with her mother. They were so poor that sometimes they had no food to eat.

One day, the little girl went into the woods to see if she could find any nuts or berries. She was so hungry and weak, she sat down on a tree stump and began to cry.

"My dear, what is the matter?" asked a kindly voice. An old lady was smiling down at her. "Don't worry," said the stranger kindly, when she heard the little girl's story, "take this pot. It is magic. When you want to eat, simply say, 'Little pot, little pot, porridge, please!' When you want it to stop, say, 'Little pot, little pot, stop now, please!'"

The little girl was not sure she believed in magic, but she took the pot and hurried home.

When the little girl explained about the pot, her mother looked doubtful, but said, "There is no harm in trying."

"Little pot, little pot, porridge, please!" said the little girl.

At once, the magic porridge pot became warm and began to jiggle. In a few minutes, the smell of good, hot porridge filled the room. The pot was full to the brim of the most delicious porridge the little girl had ever eaten.

"Little pot, little pot, stop, please," said the girl.

For the first time in ages, she and her mother went to bed with full bellies and smiles on their faces.

The next morning, the same thing happened.
"We don't need to worry now," said the mother.

After that, each day, the little girl asked the pot
for porridge. She had been hungry for so long, that
eating porridge at every meal did not seem bad at all.

One day, the little girl walked to a town a few miles away to visit her aunt. Towards lunchtime, her mother began to feel hungry. She wondered if the porridge pot would work if she said the magic words.

"Little pot, little pot, porridge, please!" she said. To her delight, she was soon sitting down to a big bowl of hot, tasty porridge.

Just as she was finishing, she noticed that the porridge pot was still cooking. In fact, some porridge had begun to overflow the pot.

"My goodness, I must stop it!" cried the mother. She tried to remember the words that her daughter had said.

"Little pot, little pot, no more porridge, please!" she said, but the pot kept overflowing, oozing porridge across the table.

"Little pot, little pot, that's enough porridge!" she shouted. Porridge began to pour on to the floor.

"Little pot, little pot, stop, please, stop!" cried the mother desperately. It was no good. Porridge was now flowing across the floor and out of the door!

That afternoon, the little girl returned from visiting her aunt. As she drew near the village where she lived, she heard shouting and wailing. Whatever could be the matter?

When she reached the main street, the little girl stopped in her tracks, her mouth open in surprise. The street was knee-deep in porridge! The gloopy, sticky stuff was oozing through doors and out of windows as it filled up the houses. She understood at once what must have happened.

"Help!" came a familiar voice.
Her mother was leaning out of an attic
window, as the house was filling with
porridge from bottom to top, clutching
the magic porridge pot.

The porridge was up to the little girl's
waist as she waded to the house.
She yelled as loudly as she could,
"Little pot, little pot, stop now, please!"

At once, the pot stopped overflowing
with porridge.

"Thank goodness!" cried her mother.

As you can imagine, cleaning up the village took a very long time. Farmers herded their cows along the street to help eat it up. Birds fluttered down to peck at the gooey mess. And little animals crept out of the woods to try it, too.

When everywhere was clean again, the little girl and her mother sat down, exhausted.

"It's time for supper," said the mother. "Would you like some porridge?" She began to laugh, and her daughter laughed, too. The porridge was so delicious that even now, they couldn't wait to eat some.

"Just one thing," giggled the little girl. "I'll do the cooking in future!"

Old Macdonald's Bedtime

You may have heard of a farmer called Old Macdonald. He was a very busy man, working from dawn to dusk looking after all the animals on his farm.

Old Macdonald had no trouble getting up in the morning. As the sun chased the last stars from the sky, Rufus the rooster would flap up on to the farmhouse fence, open his beak wide, and call:

Cock-a-doodle-doooo!

Going to bed was another matter.
Old Macdonald found that very difficult.
There was so much work to do, he never
wanted to stop when it was time to sleep.
The animals on the farm began to worry.

"It's not good for him," snuffled Pickle the pig to his duck
friends. "He's always yawning. Our farmer needs more sleep."

Doris the duck agreed. "He needs someone to tell him when it's time to go to bed," she quacked.

"Well, Rufus tells Old Macdonald when to get up," said Sam the sheep, "with a big, loud noise like an alarm clock. We could try making a soft sound to send him to sleep."

"We can sing him a lullaby,"
neighed Harriet the horse.
"I know just the right one.
We'll need to practice –
especially you, Pickle.
We don't want any
snuffling, snorting, or
snoring in our song."

"I don't snore!" protested
Pickle, but he promised to
practice very hard all the same.

All day long, wherever Old Macdonald went on the farm, he heard weird sounds. He noticed that the animals were behaving strangely.

The hens were squawking squeakily. Pickle was oinking instead of eating his dinner.

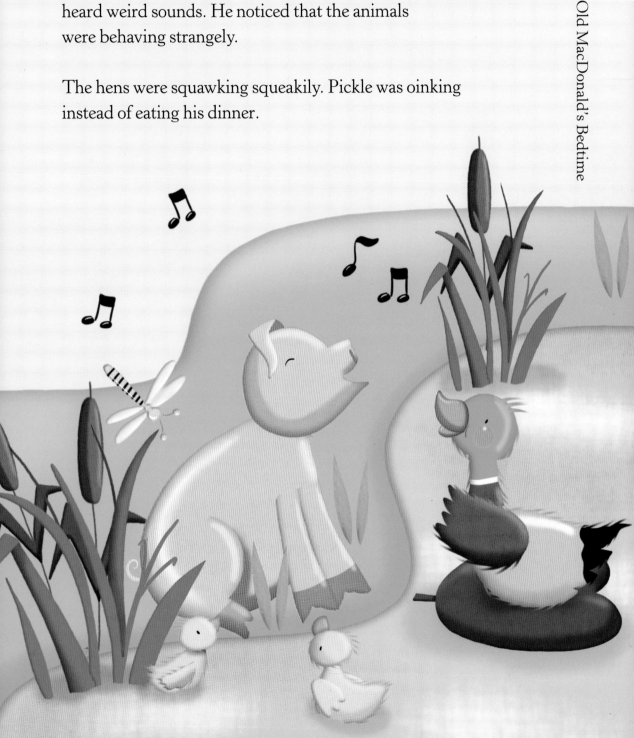

That night, Old Macdonald was working late as usual.
He was mending his old tractor in the barn.

One by one, as quietly as they could, the animals flapped
and trotted across to the open barn door.
Old Macdonald yawned and rubbed
his eyes. The animals nodded.
It was time for action.

"Ready, everyone?" whispered Doris.
"One, two, three, four…"

Very, very softly and very, very slowly, the animals sang:

Old Macdonald, time for bed!
EE–I–EE–I–O!
Time to rest your sleepy head!
EE–I–EE–I–O!
With a neigh, neigh here,
And a snuffle, snuffle there,
Here a quack, there a baa,
Everywhere a moo, moo.
Old Macdonald, time for bed!
EEEE–I–EEEE–I–OOOOOOOOO!

Old Macdonald smiled. It was time for bed. He said
goodnight to the animals and went into the farmhouse.
For the first time in ages, he was fast asleep before midnight.
All was quiet on Old Macdonald's farm, except for some
little snuffling snores … from Pickle.

The Three Little Pigs

Once upon a time, there were three little pigs who lived with their mother. The day came when they decided they were big enough and brave enough to set out to find homes of their own.

Mother Pig waved them goodbye. "Remember," she called, as the three little pigs set off down the road, "to look out for the Big, Bad Wolf."

"We will!" replied the little pigs.

It wasn't long before they met a man
with a load of straw.

"I could build a very good house
with that straw," said the first little pig.
He bought the straw and said goodbye
to his brother and sister, who tramped
on down the road.

The first little pig worked hard. By dinner time, he had built himself a very snug little house.

The first little pig had only just gone inside when he heard a knock at the door. He peeped through the window and saw that his visitor was none other than the Big, Bad Wolf!

"Little pig, little pig, let me come in!" called the wolf in his sweetest voice (which was not very sweet at all).

The first little pig tried to sound bold and brave. "No, no, by the hair on my chinny chin chin, I will *not* let you in!"

"Then I'll huff, and I'll puff, and I'll blow your house down!" growled the wolf.

The Big, Bad Wolf took a deep breath. He *huffed* and he *puffed* and he blew the house down! The first little pig ran off as fast as his trotters could carry him.

Meanwhile, the second and third little pigs had walked
on down the winding road. Soon they met a man with
a load of sticks.

"I could make myself a very good house with those sticks,"
said the second little pig.

He bought all the sticks, waved goodbye to his sister, and set to
work. Before long, he had built a snug little house.

The second little pig was just settling down for the night when there came a knock at the door. It was the first little pig!

"Let me in!" he cried. "The Big, Bad Wolf is close behind me!"

No sooner was the little pig safe inside than there came a fierce shout: "Little pigs, little pigs, let me come in!"

"No, no, by the hair on our chinny chin chins," replied the two little pigs, "we will *not* let you in!"

"Then I'll huff, and I'll puff, and I'll blow your house down!"

The Big, Bad Wolf took a deep breath and he *huffed* …

and he *puffed* …

… and he blew the house down!

It was hard work. While the Big, Bad Wolf was too out of breath to run, the two little pigs scuttled off down the road to find their sister.

She had also had a busy day. Soon after saying goodbye to her brother, she had met a man with a cart full of bricks.

"With those bricks, I could make a beautiful house," she said. She bought the whole load and set to work. Before the moon had risen in the sky, she was sitting before her own fire, feeling warm and safe.

Suddenly, there came a hammering at the door. "Let us in, let us in!" cried her brothers. "The Big, Bad Wolf is on his way!"

"We'll see about that!" said the third little pig. She let her brothers in and locked the door.

It wasn't long before they heard the wolf outside. "Little pigs, little pigs, let me come in!"

"No, no, by the hair on our chinny chin chins," chorused the three little pigs, "we will *not* let you in!"

"Then I'll huff, and I'll puff, and I'll blow your house down!" fumed the wolf.

He *huffed* and he *puffed*. The brick house stood strong and true. The wolf tried again. He *huffed* and he *puffed* and he *puffed* and he *huffed*! But it was no good.

Now the wolf was really angry. He couldn't blow the house down. The door was locked and the windows were closed.

Then he had an idea…

"He's trying to climb down the chimney!" whispered the
girl pig. "Help me with this pot!"

The pigs dragged a huge pot onto the fire and filled it with
water. By the time the wolf had squeezed himself down the
chimney, the pot was boiling merrily. The wolf landed in the
fireplace and scalded his tail in the boiling water.

"Yeeeeeeeeeeowwwwww!" he yelled. That Big, Bad
Wolf shot straight up the chimney and off down the road. He
was never seen again, and the three little pigs lived happily
ever after.

The Perfect Pirate

O nce upon a time, a pirate family lived in a tumbledown cottage near the sea. They were Pa Pirate, Ma Pirate, and little Petey Pirate.

Ma and Pa Pirate were feared from one shore of the Swirly Sea to the other. They hoped that little Petey would grow up to be a perfect pirate, too. When he was only a baby, they began to teach him pirate ways.

"Say 'Aaaaaaaarrrgh!' Petey," begged Ma Pirate.

"Doo doo, da da!" cooed little Petey.

Ma and Pa looked at each other. "He's very young," said Ma Pirate. "We must give him time."

But as little Petey grew, he didn't become more fearsome. He was a well-mannered child, always smiling. Ma and Pa were upset that their beloved son seemed far too polite to be a proper pirate.

"Petey, how many times do I have to tell you?" his father would say. "You don't put your goblet away on the shelf like that. Hurl it on the floor like this!"

"But that makes a mess," said Petey.

As he grew up, Petey loved reading, nature, drawing, music, and dancing. He showed no interest at all in fighting, stealing treasure, or going to bed with his seaboots on.

Ma and Pa Pirate had a serious talk.

"There's only one thing to do," said Pa Pirate. "We must take him on a voyage. The boy has pirate blood. When he's on the deck of a ship, with a fierce sou'westerly blowing in his ears, he'll know he is a pirate."

"I agree," said Ma. "We'll take Old Bartholomew's treasure map with us and look for his buried booty."

"I've never been able to make head nor tail of that map," confessed Pa Pirate, "but we can have another go."

So Ma and Pa Pirate packed up their belongings (well, other people's belongings really), cleaned their cutlasses, and stowed everything away on board their ship, the *Seahorse*.

The pirate parents loved being at sea again. They stomped around the deck, crying, "Avast me hearties!" and "Sluice me scuppers!" Petey curled up on the deck, looking pale.

After a few days, Petey stopped feeling seasick and took an interest – in studying shipworms and drawing clouds.

"It's no good," sighed Pa. "I'm sorry to say it, but our boy will never be a proper pirate. He can't do even the simplest dastardly deed, and our parrot would be more use in a fight."

"Never mind," said Ma Pirate, "let's cheer ourselves up by looking for Old Bartholomew's treasure. Now, where's that map?"

It was the parrot who found the map in the end. Unfortunately, Ma and Pa Pirate hadn't one idea in their heads about map-reading. They had spent many happy years searching for hidden treasure, but they had never found so much as a single doubloon.

Ma and Pa looked at the treasure map, scratching their heads. At last, Pa swung the ship's wheel around toward the east. Young Petey Pirate took a break from worm study and went over to see what they were doing.

"You've got the map the wrong way up," Petey told his mother. "And you're going in the wrong direction," he said to his father.

"How do you know?" spluttered Pa Pirate.

Petey explained. He used words that Ma and Pa had never heard of, such as latitude, longitude, and longshore drift.

Ma and Pa looked at each other. They knew their chance of finding the treasure was very small. Following Petey's advice couldn't make things worse.

"All right, son," said Pa Pirate. "I'll give you a week."

Petey Pirate didn't need a week. Two days later, the Pirate family was sitting on the beach of a tiny island. The Pirate parents gazed open-mouthed at the cascade of sparkling jewels tumbling from Old Bartholomew's sea chest.

"I don't believe it!" gasped Pa Pirate. "We're rich!"
Ma Pirate gave Petey a hug. "Our Petey may not be
fearsome, or quick with a cutlass," she said, "but he's the
best treasure-finder in all of the Swirly Sea, and *that*
means he is a *perfect* pirate."

The Little Red Hen

There was once a little red hen who lived with her friends on a farm. One day, the little red hen found some ears of wheat that had fallen from the farmer's truck. She didn't eat them at once, for as soon as she saw them, she had an idea.

"Who will help me plant this wheat?" she asked her friends.

"Well, I won't," said the cat.

"Nor will I," said the rat.

"I simply can't," said the pig.

"Then I'll do it myself," said the little red hen. And she did.

The tiny grains of wheat grew little green shoots, then strong, tall stems. At the top, ears of wheat slowly ripened in the sun. At last, the little red hen saw that the wheat was ready to be cut.

"Who will help me harvest the wheat?" she asked.

"Well, I won't," said the cat.

"Nor will I," said the rat.

"I simply can't," said the pig.

"Then I'll do it myself," said the little red hen. And she did.

When she had cut all the wheat and put it in a sack, the little red hen went to her friends again.

"Who will help me take the wheat to the mill to be ground into flour?" she asked.

"Well, I won't," said the cat.

"Nor will I," said the rat.

"I simply can't," said the pig.

"Then I'll do it myself," said the little red hen. And she did. When the miller had ground the wheat into flour, the little red hen took it back to the farm.

FLOUR

"Who will help me make some bread with this flour?"
she asked her friends.

"Well, I won't," said the cat.

"Nor will I," said the rat.

"I simply can't," said the pig.

"Then I'll do it myself," said the little red hen. And she did.

Soon a wonderful smell came from the
farmhouse kitchen. The bread was ready!

The little red hen appeared at the farmhouse door. She called to her friends, who were relaxing in the sunshine.

"Who will help me to eat my delicious bread?" called the little red hen.

"Well, I will!" said the cat.

"So will I!" said the rat.

"I simply can't wait!" said the pig.

The little red hen saw that the cat, the rat, and the pig were not really friends at all.

"No," she said, "I think I'll eat it myself." And she did.

Beauty and the Beast

Once a rich merchant had three daughters. They were all very pretty, but the older girls only thought about themselves. The youngest, named Beauty, was kind and helpful. Her father loved her best of all.

One day, the merchant came home early. The girls could see at once that something was wrong. "I have lost all my money," he said. "We will have to leave our grand house."

The older girls were horrified to find themselves in a tiny cottage with no servants. While they complained, Beauty set to work to make the little house clean and comfortable.

The merchant needed to visit a far away town on business. "What would you like me to bring you home, my dears?" he asked.

"Diamonds!" cried the eldest girl at once.

"Pearls!" replied her sister, just as quickly.

Beauty saw her father's worried face and said, "I would love some white roses, please."

She was the only one to wave him goodbye.

The merchant's business went
well. He couldn't wait to get
home, but as night fell, he
found himself lost in a forest.

At last, in the distance, he saw a
light and was amazed to find a
huge palace. The door was open
wide, but there was nobody
in sight.

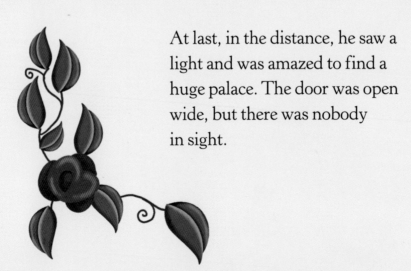

"Hello?" called the merchant, as he went inside. Still
nobody came, but he found a room with a blazing fire
and a delicious meal on the table. He was so hungry
that he sat down and ate. Later, feeling warm and full,
he found an empty bedroom and went to sleep.

When the merchant awoke, the sun
was shining and birds were singing
outside. He went out into the beautiful
gardens around the palace.

The sight of a large rose bush, covered with white flowers, reminded him of Beauty. Reaching out his hand, he picked a single rose.

At once, there was a terrible roar behind him. "You thief!" bellowed a deafening voice. "How dare you steal from me?"

The man turned and saw a fearful Beast glaring at him. "Please do not kill me," begged Beauty's father, falling to his knees. "What can I give you instead of my life?"

"In one month," growled the Beast, "you must return, bringing whoever you first meet when you arrive home."

Stuttering his thanks, the merchant hurried home. He was horrified when, a mile from his door, he saw Beauty coming to meet him. Sadly, he told her of his promise.

"A promise must be kept," said Beauty.
At the end of one month, she went with
her father to the palace in the forest.

As before, the door was open and dinner was on the table.
It was not long before the Beast appeared. Beauty tried not
to be afraid. When the Beast spoke, his voice was gentle.

"Don't worry," he said, "you will not be harmed."

Once again, Beauty and her father were parted. The Beast showed the lovely girl to her room and left her.

Beauty was amazed by the rich, luxurious clothes and furnishings that had been prepared for her. On the wall there was a strange mirror with symbols underneath it. Beauty looked at them and wondered what they could mean.

Soon Beauty became used to living in the palace. During the day, she was alone, free to paint, read, or walk in the gardens. In the evening, the Beast joined her for dinner and they talked together. In time, Beauty and the Beast became close friends.

One day, as she stood in front of the mirror, Beauty thought of home. "I wish I could see my dear father again," she sighed. To her amazement, she saw him in the mirror. He was lying in bed and looked very ill.

"Please let me go home to see my father," Beauty begged the Beast that evening. "I will return in one week, I promise."

The Beast was afraid he would never see her again, but he gave her a magic ring, saying, "When you are ready to return, put this on your bedside table. It will bring you back to me."

The return of his beloved daughter soon helped the merchant to feel better. After a week, he asked Beauty to stay a little longer. That night, in her dreams, she saw the Beast. He was lying on the ground near the roses, looking heartbroken. When she woke up, Beauty knew at once what she must do. She placed the magic ring on her bedside table.

When Beauty found herself again at the Beast's palace, she ran at once into the garden. There, beside the rose bush, the Beast lay on the ground. Tears came to Beauty's eyes as she sat beside him.

"Oh Beast," she whispered, "please don't die. You are my best friend and I love you."

As she spoke, something extraordinary happened. The Beast transformed … into a handsome Prince!

He took Beauty's hands in his.
"A wicked fairy put a spell on me,"
he said. "Only true love could save me."

Beauty's father was overjoyed to see his
daughter's happiness, and even her sisters
smiled on her wedding day.

The Lion and the Mouse

Once a little mouse was scampering through the jungle when he bumped into something big and yellow.

"Eeek!" squeaked the little mouse.

"Rrrrrrroar!" replied the big, yellow thing. It was a lion!

The little mouse turned to run away as fast as his tiny feet could carry him, but the lion stretched out his paw and put it down firmly on the mouse's tail.

"Not so fast, Little Mouse," growled the lion. "You'll make a tasty afternoon snack."

"Oh please, please, Sir," squeaked the mouse, "don't eat me. I promise, if you let me go, I will be your friend and help you whenever you need me."

The lion roared with laughter. "When would I ever need *you?*" he chortled. "But you've cheered me up today, so go on your way, Little Mouse."

"Thank you, my friend," replied the mouse.

The very next day, as the lion was snoozing after lunch, some hunters crept up and captured him in a net. Although he roared and fought with all his strength, the mighty beast could not get free.

"We'll leave him here tonight," said the hunters, "and take him away in the morning."

The hunters left. Night fell, and the exhausted lion lay still. Suddenly, he heard a tiny sound. "I knew you would need me one day, my friend," whispered the little mouse.

"I am much bigger and stronger than you," sighed the lion, "and I couldn't get free. What could you possibly do?"

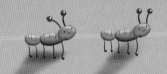

"Only this," smiled the mouse, and he began to gnaw at the ropes holding the net to the ground. Very quickly, his sharp little teeth cut them in two. In minutes, the lion was free.

From then on, the lion and the mouse were good friends. Even the strongest person needs a friend sometimes; no matter what their size, a friend can make a BIG difference.

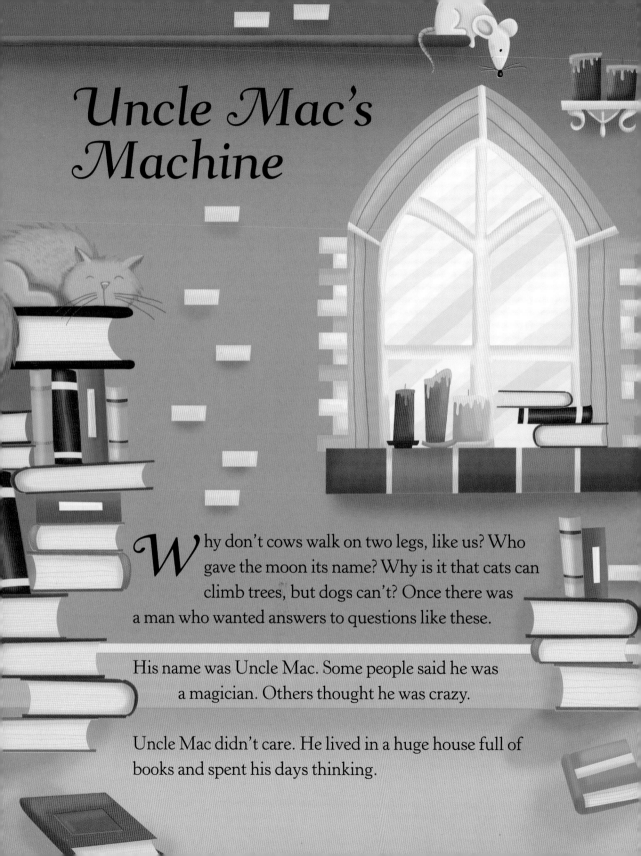

Uncle Mac's Machine

Why don't cows walk on two legs, like us? Who gave the moon its name? Why is it that cats can climb trees, but dogs can't? Once there was a man who wanted answers to questions like these.

His name was Uncle Mac. Some people said he was a magician. Others thought he was crazy.

Uncle Mac didn't care. He lived in a huge house full of books and spent his days thinking.

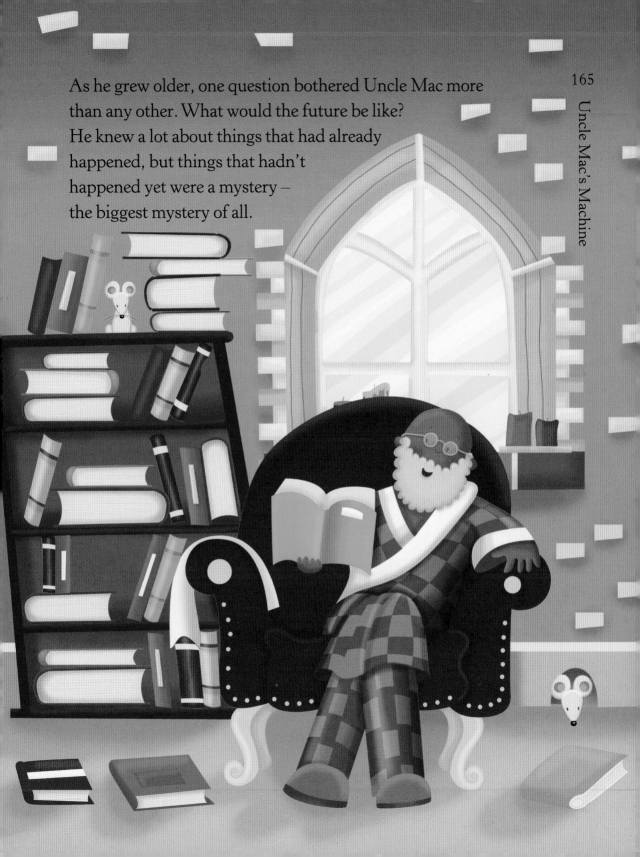

As he grew older, one question bothered Uncle Mac more than any other. What would the future be like? He knew a lot about things that had already happened, but things that hadn't happened yet were a mystery – the biggest mystery of all.

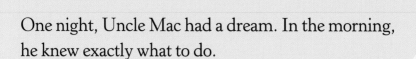

One night, Uncle Mac had a dream. In the morning, he knew exactly what to do.

He made an announcement to his cat, who was the only creature he could rely on to listen. "Fluffikins," he said, "I am going to build a Time Machine! It is the only way to find out what will happen in the future."

After his usual breakfast of eggs, oranges, and spaghetti, he set to work.

First, he made a plan …

Then, he collected what he needed …
Finally, he began to build his machine.

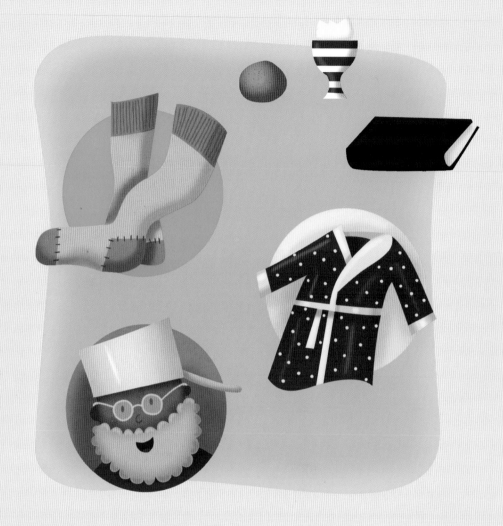

Several years and huge amounts of eggs, oranges, and spaghetti later, he attached the last sprocket, wound up the wishing wheel, and pressed the seriously-silly switch. He was ready.

What does an inventor wear for a visit to the future?
Uncle Mac chose purple socks and a red robe with blue spots.
He put a saucepan on his head for protection.

"Ready, Fluffikins?" asked Uncle Mac.

Fluffikins put his paw on the launch lever.

"To the future!" cried the amazing inventor.

"*Meeow!*" replied his furry assistant.

With a *whiz* and a *flash*,
Uncle Mac ... disappeared.

Fluffikins did not know how long
an inventor might be away when
journeying into the future. In fact,
it was only an hour later that Uncle
Mac returned to his big, old house.
He walked up his own drive, whistling.

Back in the house, he sat down in a comfy armchair and smiled. The man who had always been busy wondering and planning just sat there, smiling. Fluffikins jumped up onto his lap and began to purr.

News of the change in Uncle Mac reached the nearby village.
People began to visit to see him for themselves.

"A Time Machine?" they cried, when he explained.
"Impossible! If you really went to the future,
what was it like?"

"Well," said Uncle Mac, "one day, people will whiz about
in metal boxes. They will talk to friends who are miles away.
They will make warm rain fall in their houses. They will have
machines to wash their clothes. And best of all, they still have
eggs and oranges and spaghetti."

"What nonsense!" said a baker to his friend the farmer. "I knew he was crazy."

"Ridiculous!" cried the farmer. "He'll tell us that there will be machines for milking cows next."

The people went on their way, muttering, and Uncle Mac went back to his books, a happy man. He knew that the future was full of wonderful things. And no one needs a Time Machine to get there. It will come along all by itself.

Town Mouse and Country Mouse

Among the roots of an old oak tree lived
a little mouse called Percy. He loved his
snug, warm home. It suited him perfectly.

One day, Percy's cousin Cecil came to stay. He lived
in a busy town not far away. Percy was looking forward
to his visit, but from the moment he arrived,
Cecil found things to complain about.

"This mud is awful," he moaned.
"And look at all these leaves everywhere.
How can you live somewhere so untidy?"

"Come inside," said Percy. "And have something
to eat. You must be hungry after your journey."

"Well, perhaps I could manage some pizza
and a fizzy drink," sighed Cecil.

"Er ... it's blackberries and mint tea,"
said Percy.

Cecil shuddered.

Later, when it was dark, Percy gave Cecil a candle and led him to his room. Cecil didn't like the way the candle made flickering, spooky shadows.

"Haven't you heard of electricity?" he asked.

In the middle of the night, Percy was woken by a shriek. He hurried to his cousin.

"This house is haunted! There's a terrible creaking, moaning sound," sobbed Cecil.

"I can't hear anything," a puzzled Percy replied. Then he smiled. "It's just my old tree swaying in the wind," he said. "It's a lovely sound."

Next morning, Cecil complained that he had hardly slept at all.

"Let's go for a walk," Percy said.

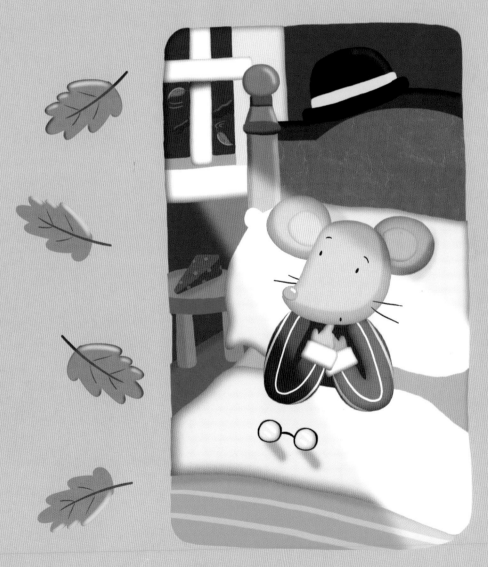

It wasn't a great success. Cecil complained about long grass, insects, and the cold. On the way home, Cecil suddenly shouted, "HELP! There's a monster behind the hedge!"

Percy peeped through the brambles. "It's a cow," he said. "You're not enjoying yourself, are you, Cecil?"

"I'm sorry, Percy," Cecil replied, "this is not the place for me. I'm going back to town this afternoon. Why don't you come with me? You'll wonder why you lived here so long."

When the pair reached the town,
Percy was amazed by the tall
buildings and the traffic.

"It's so noisy!" he yelled. "I can't
hear myself think!"

"Nonsense!" shouted Cecil. "It's
just lively. Look out, Percy!"

He pulled Percy out of the path of
a car just in time.

Cecil's home was inside the wall of a grand house. He proudly showed Percy his electric light, his running water, and his heating system.

"You don't have a kitchen," said Percy.

"No need!" smiled Cecil. "There's always plenty of food."

Cecil took Percy to the pantry of the house and scampered up on to the shelves. "What will you have, Percy?" he asked. "Apple pie? Cream? Cake? A little cheese?"

Percy was not used to such rich food. He could only eat a little.

As they strolled back down a long, carpeted corridor, Cecil suddenly squeaked, "Quick! Run for your life! This way!"

He set off at an incredible pace, with Percy panting behind.

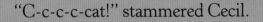

"What is it?" cried Percy as they scurried into Cecil's home.

"C-c-c-c-cat!" stammered Cecil.

"But how did she get in?" asked Percy.

"She didn't," replied Cecil. "She lives here, too. I have to watch out for her *all the time.*"

Hole
Sweet Hole

Percy didn't sleep well that night. Dreams of thundering traffic and prowling cats made him restless. The next morning he packed his bag.

"It's been … interesting," he told Cecil, "but I feel more comfortable in my home, just as you feel more comfortable in yours."

That night, safe in his own little house,
Percy sat down to write to his cousin.
"Visiting is fun," he wrote, "but there
really is no place like home."

The Castle of Dreams

Far away and long ago, a Princess sat by an open window, looking worried and sad. An old woman was walking past under the window. She was carrying a basket of flowers. She looked up and caught sight of the Princess's beautiful face. "What is it that makes you so unhappy, my child?" she asked.

The Princess thought for a moment, then she said, "I am a Princess. I have dresses and jewels. Servants do whatever I ask. Many girls dream of being me. But I have no dream of my own. I have everything I want, but I am not happy."

The old woman smiled kindly. "Everyone needs dreams," she said, "even you. Tonight, when you go to sleep, put this flower under your pillow and see what happens."

That night, in her beautiful bedchamber, the Princess did as the old woman had said. Almost as soon as her eyes were closed, she began to dream. She found herself in a strange country, floating towards a gleaming castle on a hilltop. As she reached the doorway, someone came to meet her.

"Welcome to the Castle of Dreams," said the old woman. "Come inside and see which dream is right for you."

Inside the castle there were many doors. "Try one," said the old woman.

The Princess opened the nearest door and found herself in a beautiful garden. A handsome young Prince turned towards her and held out his arms. "Ah, there you are, my love," he said. "I have been waiting for you for so very long."

The Princess moved forward, but instead of finding herself in the Prince's arms, she found herself back outside the door she had just entered.

There was only one thing to be done. She opened the nearest door and went inside. Three little children, with golden curls ran towards her. "Mamma!" they cried. "Come and read us a story!" The Princess sat down on a little bed, while they all cuddled around her, soft and warm. She opened a book … and found herself back outside again.

"I'm beginning to see how this works," she said to herself, and once more, she opened a door.

A line of poor people, in ragged clothes and holding empty bowls, met her eyes. "Please help us," they said. The Princess ran forward immediately to do what she could and found herself once more outside the door.

In the next room, a party was in full swing. Girls and boys were dancing. As the Princess entered, they all turned to her and cried, "She's here! Now the party can really begin!" But as the Princess began to tap her foot to the music, she found herself back outside the door.

The Princess tried many doors. She swam in the sea with dolphins. She planted flowers in a beautiful garden. She swept a floor on her hands and knees, something she had never done before. She settled on a sofa, and began to read an exciting book. She stood on a hill and gazed at the stars.

Always, she stayed only for a moment – just enough to want to stay longer.

Then, suddenly, the Princess found herself outside the castle again. The old woman was there, too. "Did you find a dream?" she asked. "Many dreams," smiled the Princess. "Must I only choose one?"

"Of course not," replied the old woman. "You can have as many dreams as you wish, and they can all come true, one way or another."

The Princess closed her eyes. When she opened them, she was back in her bed in the palace, already looking foward to all the wonderful dreams she could follow.

She never saw the old woman again, and sometimes the Princess wondered if perhaps she had been a dream as well.

The Three Billy Goats Gruff

High in the mountains, there lived three billy goats called Gruff. One day, they set off to find some sweet, green grass to eat. They trotted down the mountainside until they came to a valley with a river running through it. On the other side of the river was a meadow of the sweetest, greenest grass they had ever seen.

There was a rickety wooden bridge over the river, but the billy goats Gruff knew that under the bridge lived an ugly old troll. Whenever he heard footsteps overhead, he would leap out and gobble up anyone who dared try to cross.

The three billy goats Gruff wondered what to do. Then the smallest billy goat had an idea and set off towards the river. *Trip, trap, trip, trap,* went his hoofs on the wooden bridge.

At once, the troll jumped out from underneath. "Who's that trip-trapping over my bridge?" he roared.

The smallest billy goat Gruff trembled. "It's me," he said, "I'm off to the meadow to eat the sweet, green grass."

"Oh no, you're not," bellowed the troll. "I'm going to eat you up!"

"Please don't!" cried the smallest billy goat. "My brother is coming along next. He's much fatter and tastier than me."

"Off you go then!" yelled the troll. "I can wait."

The smallest billy goat Gruff trotted off into the meadow and began to eat the sweet, green grass. A minute later, the second billy goat Gruff's hoofs could be heard going *trip, trap, trip, trap,* across the wooden bridge.

Once again, the troll jumped out. "Who's that trip-trapping over my bridge?" he roared.

The second billy goat Gruff replied boldly. "It's me," he said, "I'm off to the meadow to eat the sweet, green grass."

"Oh no, you're not," bellowed the troll. "I'm going to eat you!"

"Don't!" cried the second billy goat. "My big brother will be here soon. He'll be much tastier!"

"All right!" the troll yelled. "Go on your way!"

The second billy goat Gruff galloped off into the meadow to join his little brother and eat the sweet, green grass. At last, the biggest billy goat Gruff set off across the bridge. *TRIP, TRAP, TRIP, TRAP,* went his mighty hoofs.

The troll jumped out from under the bridge. "I've been waiting for you!" he roared. "I'm going to eat you up!"

"Oh, no you're not!" bellowed the biggest billy goat.

TRIP, TRAP, TRIP, TRAP, the biggest billy goat Gruff thundered across the bridge. He lowered his head and butted the troll with his huge horns. *BOOMF!* The troll flew up into the air and down into the river. *SPLASH!*

The three billy goats Gruff ate the sweet, green grass and grew bigger every day. The troll was never seen again.

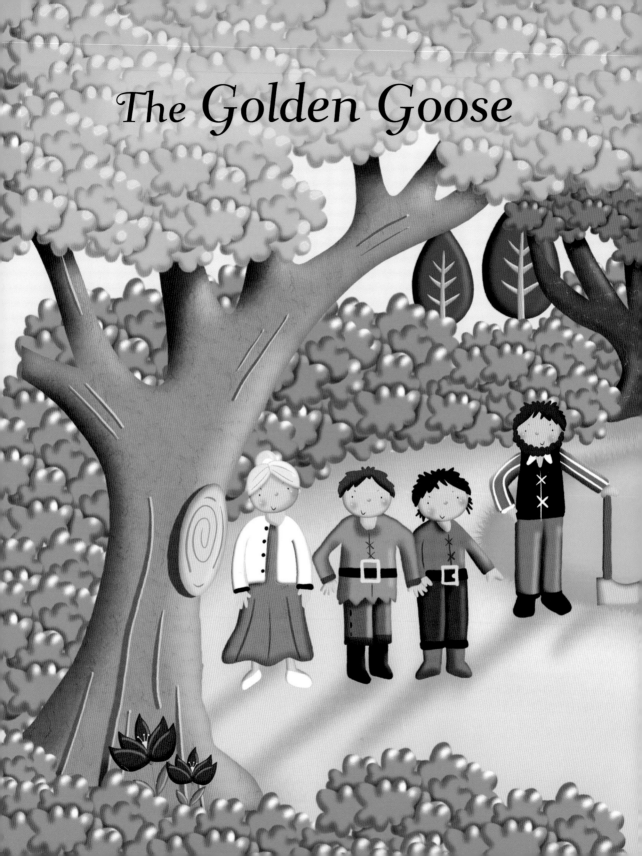

The Golden Goose

Once a woodcutter and his wife had three sons. They loved the two older boys, but for some reason they only ever made fun of the youngest.

One day, the eldest boy went into the forest to chop some wood. His mother gave him some cakes and milk for his lunch. To his surprise, when he sat down to eat and drink, a little man appeared beside him.

"I'm hungry and thirsty," said the little man.
"Could I have a cake and some milk?"

"Of course not!" laughed the eldest son.
"I won't have enough for myself if you do!"

The little man said nothing and went away, but a few
minutes later the eldest son tripped over a log and hurt
his ankle. He hobbled home, unable to finish his work.

The next day, he still couldn't walk, so the middle son went to the forest instead. He had cakes and milk for his lunch, too.

No sooner had the middle son sat down at lunchtime than the little man appeared. "I'm hungry and thirsty," he said. "Could I have a cake and some milk?"

"No!" said the middle son.
"Why should I give you my food?"

Once again, the little man went away, but a few minutes later, a branch fell on the middle son's shoulder, and he was not able to carry on working that day or the next.

"I'll go instead!" said the youngest son. Everyone laughed. "You'd be hopeless!" they jeered, but he was determined. His mother gave him some stale bread and water.

After a morning's work, the youngest son sat down to eat.
At once, the little man appeared. "I'm hungry and thirsty,"
he said. "Could I have a cake and some milk?"

"I'm sorry, I don't have any," replied the youngest son, "but
you can share my bread and water if you like."

After they had finished eating, the little man said, "You
deserve a reward. Chop down that tree over there to find it."

With that, the little man disappeared,
never to be seen again.

The youngest son set to work to cut down
the tree. As it fell, he saw that the trunk
was hollow, and inside was a goose, with
feathers of pure gold.

Tucking the goose under his arm, the youngest son decided not to go home, where he was not wanted, but to set off into the wide world.

"My golden goose will make me rich and famous," he said to himself. And it did.

Bertrand the Bold

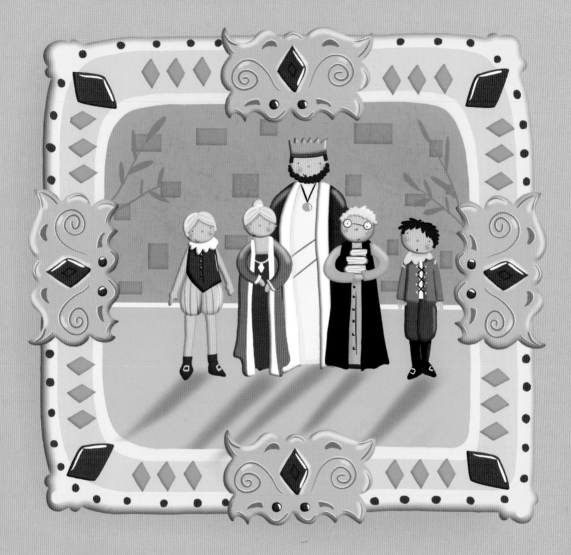

K ing Tarquin the Tall and his wife had three sons:
Clarence the Clever, Philip the Fast, and Bertrand
the Bold. As you can see, King Tarquin the Tall
lived up to his name. He really was *tall*.

Clarence the Clever spent most of his time reading or having Serious Thoughts. He really was very *clever*.

Philip the Fast boasted that he could run around the castle more quickly than his horse. It is true that his horse was rather old and slow, but still, Philip certainly was *fast*.

But Bertrand the Bold was not bold. He was not even the tiniest bit brave. He jumped at loud noises. He was scared of spiders. He was shy with strangers. He did not live up to his name in any way at all.

One evening, just as the sun was setting, King Tarquin the Tall received news that someone had set fire to his fields of barley. He looked out over the battlements and saw flames racing across the golden crop. Who on earth would dare to do such a thing?

Soon news arrived. "A dragon
has been sighted, your Highness,"
gasped a farmer. "He has been eating my
sheep and breathing on my house."

"Breathing?" queried the King.

"Breathing fire, your Highness. The
dreadful animal set light to my roof!" the
farmer explained.

Now the King understood why his barley was burning.
He summoned his sons.

"Lads," he said, "our kingdom is threatened, and it is up to
you to face this terrible foe. Clarence, you are the eldest, you
must go first."

"Ah," said Clarence, "yes,
well, now, you see, I have
read widely on the habits
of dragons, and I really feel
that we should simply ask
him to go away. Dragons
are very clever. He will
certainly understand our
point of view."

"Nonsense!" said the
King. "What he will
certainly understand is the
point of a sharp sword!"

The King turned to his second son. "Philip," he said firmly, "it looks as if you must go."

"I would love to, of course," said Philip the Fast, "but surely, Father, that's not wise with my injury."

"What injury?" demanded the King.

Philip hobbled a few steps. "I pulled a muscle while running," he said. "The pain is dreadful."

With a sinking heart, King Tarquin the Tall turned to his youngest son. "That only leaves you, Bertrand," he said.

Bertrand was dreadfully frightened of dragons. But at that moment, face face with the King, he was even more frightened of his father.

"I will go, Sire," he cried.

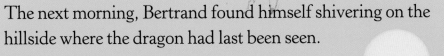

The next morning, Bertrand found himself shivering on the hillside where the dragon had last been seen.

It was not long before the dragon appeared. It was huge and it was hungry.

Bertrand hid behind a nearby rock, but the dragon really was clever. It came nearer and peered down, right into Bertrand's face.

Bertrand gulped. He felt sure that at any moment he would be flame-grilled and served up for breakfast.

Bertrand shut his eyes and waited for the worst. Suddenly he became aware that he could hardly feel the dragon's breath on his face, but something was tickling his hand.

Bertrand glanced down and spotted the biggest spider he had ever seen strolling towards his thumb.

"Aaaaaaaarrrrrggghhh!" yelled Bertrand.

"Aaaaaaaarrrrrggghhh!" screeched the dragon, frightened out of its wits by the sudden sound.

A foe brave enough to scream his war-cry in the face of danger gave the dragon second thoughts about breakfast. He headed for the hills, never to be seen again.

Bertrand the Bold went home to a hero's welcome.
The dragon had gone. The spider had scuttled away.
Bertrand was far too scared to speak about what had
happened. So no one ever found out the real story of his
battle with the dragon.

Except you, of course.

The Enormous Turnip

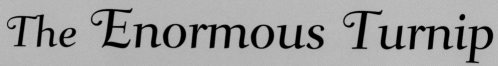

Once upon a time, an old man and an old woman
lived in a little cottage with lots of space outside it.
The old man loved to grow vegetables, and the old
woman loved to cook them. They *both* loved to eat them!

One sunny morning in spring, the old man pulled on his gardening boots and went outside to plant some seeds. He had already prepared the soil, so it did not take him long to sprinkle the tiny seeds in careful rows.

"We'll soon have some tasty turnips to eat," he told his wife.

"I can't wait!" said the old woman.

Over the next few days, the sun shone and gentle rain fell on the garden. Before long, tiny green shoots could be seen above the ground. The shoots became small, green turnip leaves. Each day, they grew a little more, and under the soil, the turnip roots grew as well.

Before long, the young turnips were big enough to eat. The old man gathered a few each day, but one turnip seemed to be growing faster than the others.

"I'm going to leave that one," the old man told his wife. "It's so big it might win a prize."

The old man took great care of his prize turnip. He gave it special fertilizer and watered it during dry spells.

The turnip grew and grew.

"I've never seen a turnip
like it," said the old man.
"I'll pull it up soon. It will
take ages to clean up a vast
vegetable like that."

Still the turnip grew.
The old man began to
wonder if it would fit in
his wheelbarrow.

The morning came at last when the old man went out to pull up the turnip. It was so big, he didn't have to bend to grasp the leaves. Taking a firm hold, he leaned back and *pulled*.

The turnip didn't budge.
The old woman was watching from the window. She hurried out to help her husband.

"One, two, three, *pull!*"
shouted the old man.
But the turnip didn't move.

The old man and the old woman heaved until they were exhausted. It was no good.

Just then, a boy came strolling along the lane at the bottom of the garden.

"Will you come and help us pull up this enormous turnip?" called the old man.

"Easy!" replied the boy. He jumped over the fence and held onto the old woman.

"One, two, three, *pull!*" shouted the old woman.

The old man, the old woman, and the boy *pulled* with all their might. But they could not budge the turnip.

A girl came past on her way to school.

"Will you come and help us *pull* up this enormous turnip?" called the old man.

"One, two, three, *pull!*" cried the boy.

The old man, the old woman, the boy, and the girl *pulled*. It was no good.

The boy spotted a dog in the meadow. He whistled, and the dog came bounding over to help.

"Careful!" said the girl, as the dog got hold of her skirt with his mouth. "One, two, three, *pull!*"

The old man, the old woman, the boy, the girl, and the dog *pulled*. The turnip stayed stuck.

"Here, Puss!" called the girl, seeing a cat walking along the fence.

Down jumped the cat and took hold of the dog's tail.

"Woof, woof, woof, *woof!*" barked the dog.

The old man, the old woman, the boy, the girl, the dog, and the cat *pulled*. It was hopeless.

Just then, the cat spotted a little mouse who had been watching right from the beginning. The little mouse scampered forward and took hold of the cat's tail.

"Meeow, meeow, meeow, *meeow!*" cried the cat, and everyone understood what that meant!

The old man, the old woman, the boy, the girl, the dog, the cat, and the mouse *pulled* … and all of a sudden, the turnip popped out of the ground and everyone went flying.

Now everyone could see that it was the most *enormous* turnip that had ever been grown.

Of course, the turnip *did* win a prize. At the end of the day, the old man, the old woman, the boy, the girl, the dog, the cat, and the mouse sat down together to eat it. They all agreed on one thing: it was *enormously* delicious!

The Hare and the Tortoise

Nobody would say that Tortoise was a speedy animal. Whatever he was doing, he took his time.

Hare was just the opposite. He was always in a rush, scampering here and there and not looking where he was going.

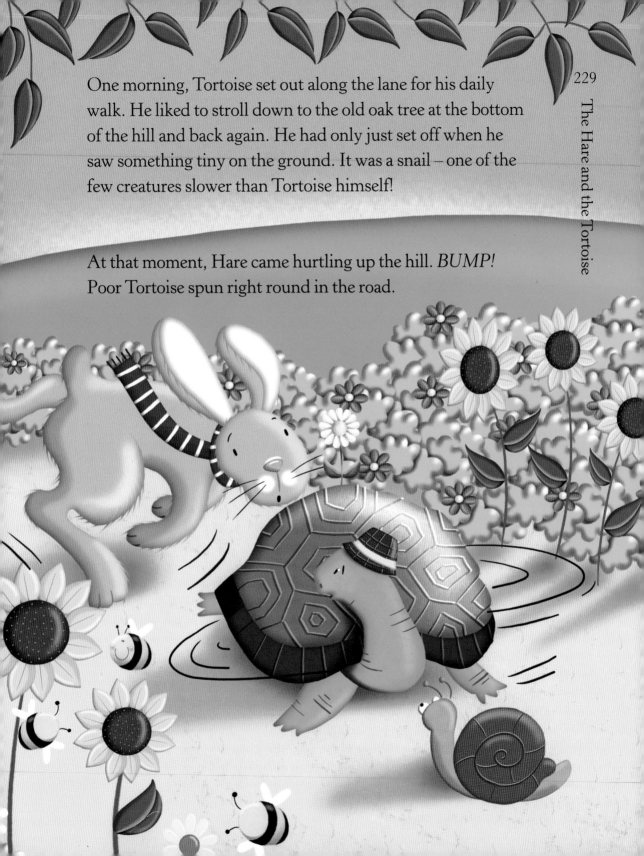

One morning, Tortoise set out along the lane for his daily walk. He liked to stroll down to the old oak tree at the bottom of the hill and back again. He had only just set off when he saw something tiny on the ground. It was a snail — one of the few creatures slower than Tortoise himself!

At that moment, Hare came hurtling up the hill. *BUMP!* Poor Tortoise spun right round in the road.

The surprise left Hare speechless for a moment, which gave Tortoise a chance to speak up.

"You really must be more careful, Hare," he said in his usual slow way. "You'll never get anywhere rushing around like you do."

Hare laughed. "I'll get further than you, old slowpoke," he chortled. "Are you going to the oak tree? I could be there and back before you got started."

"I don't think you could, you know," said Tortoise.

"That sounds like a challenge!" yelled Hare, bouncing about in the road now. "Let's have a race!"

"Fair enough," said Tortoise, slowly.

"Ready … steady … wait for it, Hare … *go!*"

Off zoomed Hare. He was out of sight in seconds.
Tortoise plodded on, just as he always did.

Meanwhile, Hare was dashing
down the lane, so full of himself
that he jumped and skipped
as he went. By the time he
reached the oak tree,
he was out of breath.

"I'll just sit down here for a minute," said Hare to himself. "It will take Tortoise all morning to get here. I've got plenty of time."

The sun was warm. Before long, Hare began to feel drowsy. His head nodded. His long ears flopped. A little snoring sound could be heard.

When Tortoise came slowly into view an hour later, Hare was still asleep. Tortoise didn't say a word. He just kept walking.

It was lunchtime when Hare woke up. When he remembered the race, he jumped to his feet and shot off down the lane. There was no sign of Tortoise.

Hare ran faster than he had ever run before – that's pretty fast! He skidded to a stop outside Tortoise's house. To his horror, the door opened and the slow old creature appeared.

"Ah, Hare!" said Tortoise. "There you are! Would you like some carrot cake?"

"Wah? Hah? How?" panted Hare.

"Slow and steady wins the race," said Tortoise, slowly and steadily. "Come on in."

The carrot cake was delicious. Hare managed to sit still for five whole minutes before he bounced out of his seat and said goodbye. Tortoise smiled ... and helped himself to another slice of cake.

Moon Magic

O ver the hills and far away, in the middle of a wood, there lived an owl family. They were Father Owl, Mother Owl, and Little Egg. A hole in a mighty oak tree was their home.

During the day, the owls slept, hidden from sight. At night, when the moon rose in the sky and the stars sparkled above, Father Owl and Mother Owl flew out of their home on silent wings. They swooped through the wood, looking for food.

Little Egg didn't swoop. He was safe in his shell, in a bed of feathers, in the hole, in the oak tree, in the wood.

One day, as spring slowly became summer in the woodland, the Mother Owl could hear a tiny calling sound from Little Egg. It was time for him to hatch. That night, Little Egg gently cracked open and someone very fluffy came out.

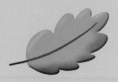

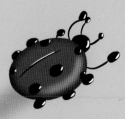

"Whoooo is this?" asked Father Owl, looking down at the bundle of fluff.

"It is Little Owl," said Mother Owl. "He is here at last."

Little Owl was snug and safe in his bed of feathers, in the hole, in the oak tree, in the wood.

Each night, Father Owl flew off to find food for them all.
When Little Owl grew bigger, he needed even more food!
Mother Owl flew off as well to find enough for the family.

When he was all alone, Little Owl began to be worried.
He wondered when his parents would come back.
He shuffled to the edge of the hole and looked out
at the woodland and up at the sky. Something big
and round was shining down at him.

"Oooooo!" said Little Owl.

When Mother Owl came home, he told her that he felt lonely and frightened without her. "And something kept looking at me," he said, "up in the sky, big and shiny."

Mother Owl hooted with laughter. "It's the mooooon," she said. "It is magic. Each night, it shines down and keeps owls safe. When I am not here, and Father Owl is not here, the magic moon will look after you."

That made Little Owl feel better. That night, he shuffled to the edge of the hole and looked up at the moon. It was looking down, making sure he was safe.

Little Owl was getting older now. He did a lot of thinking about things. After a few days, he found something new to worry about. He noticed that the moon was beginning to disappear. At first, he wasn't sure, but after a while he saw that each night there was a little bit less of the moon.

He wasn't sure if there was enough moon left to keep him safe each night.

Night by night, the moon got smaller and smaller, until it was just a silver sliver in the sky.

That night, Little Owl begged his mother not to go out.

"I have to go, Little Owl," she said, "or you will be hungry. You know that the magic moon will look after you."

"It isn't magic," said Little Owl sadly. "Something has been nibbling away at it. Last night there was hardly any moon. Tonight it won't be there at all."

"Nooooooo, Little Owl," smiled his mother. "That's why the moon is magic. Each month, it gets smaller and smaller night after night, until it is a tiny sliver. Then it begins to grow again, until one night it is big and round once more."

Little Owl wasn't sure, but he knew that his mother was very wise. Sure enough, over the next few nights the moon began to grow.

By the time the magic moon was big again, Little Owl was quite big, too. He understood lots of things now. Safe on a branch, near the hole, in the oak tree, in the wood, he smiled at the moon. And the moon smiled back.

ABOUT THE STORIES

Folk stories and fairy tales have been told to children all over the world for hundreds of years. In them, all kinds of magical things can happen: beasts become princes, boys climb beanstalks, and little girls steal porridge from bears.

They are an integral part of most people's childhoods, but they are often more than just fun stories to share at bedtime. Many of the tales collected in this book have things to teach us, and these messages have been passed down from parents to children throughout the centuries. Some of the traditional stories have also been adapted and rewritten over time and by authors in different cultures, to reflect particular ideas or interpretations.

In this part of the book you can discover all about the origins, histories, and meanings of some of the world's best-loved bedtime stories.

Jack and the Beanstalk

Jack and the Beanstalk is a traditional English fairy tale. The earliest known version of the story is a book printed in 1807 called *The History of Jack and the Bean Stalk*. However, the tale is certainly much older. For instance, a stage play, *The Story of Jack Spriggins and the Enchanted Bean*, dates from the 1730s. A version of the giant's cry, "Fee! Fie! Foe! Fum! I smell the blood of an Englishman," also appears in William Shakespeare's *King Lear* ("Fie, foh, and fum, I smell the blood of a British man").

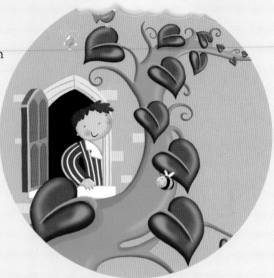

Chicken Little

The story of *Chicken Little* existed for many centuries in an oral tradition before it was published in book form in the early 19th century. There are retellings of this story all over Europe; in an early Danish language version, Chicken Little is "Kylling Kluk." In some versions, the birds are going to "tell the king" that the sky is falling down, and in others they don't have a specific reason to go on a journey. But almost every retelling ends with them getting eaten by a cunning fox!

Puss in Boots

Puss in Boots is a traditional European fairy tale. It is likely that the story existed in the oral tradition for a long time before it was printed in a book. A man called Giovanni Francesco Straparola published one of the oldest written versions of the story in an Italian collection of fairy tales in 1553. In this version, the castle belongs to a lord instead of an ogre, and the cat is a fairy in disguise!

However, it is a story by French author Charles Perrault called *Le Maître Chat, ou Le Chat Botté* ("Master Cat, or the Booted Cat") that bears closest resemblance to the version we know today. Perrault's tale was published in 1697, in a collection which included early versions of some of our most well-loved fairy stories, including *Cinderella*, *Sleeping Beauty*, *Little Red Riding Hood*, and *Blue Beard*. The book became an instant success and was translated into English in 1729.

Puss in Boots has provided inspiration for countless movies, cartoons, and stage shows ever since.

The Gingerbread Man

This story was first published in an American magazine in 1875, titled *The Gingerbread Boy*. It is likely that the tale existed before this. According to the unnamed author of the 1875 version, "A servant girl from Maine told it to my children… I asked where she found it and she said an old lady told it to her in her childhood." The tale belongs to a tradition of folk stories about runaway food. There are French and German stories about runaway pancakes, a Hungarian tale about a cheese, and a Slavic story about a boy made from bread dough.

Goldilocks and the Three Bears

In one of the earliest written versions of this tale, an old woman called "Silver Hair" sneaks into the bears' home to taste their food and try out their beds. Goldilocks didn't become the naughty little girl we know today until 1849. She became "Silver-Locks" when she was transformed from an old woman to a young girl, then "Golden Hair," and eventually, in 1904, she was christened "Goldilocks." This enduringly popular tale has been adapted into movies and even an opera!

Tom Thumb

Tom Thumb was a popular character in English folklore long before his tale was committed to print. The earliest known version of the story that we know today was published in London in 1621 – in fact, it is the first fairy tale to be printed in the English language! The original title of the tale was quite a mouthful for such a small main character: *The History of Tom Thumbe, the Little, for his small stature surnamed, King Arthur's Dwarfe: whose Life and adventures containe many strange and wonderfull accidents, published for the delight of merry Time-spenders.*

    The original tale was written for an adult audience and belongs to a tradition of folk stories that feature a character being swallowed. In early editions, Tom is swallowed by a cow, a giant, a fish, a miller, and a salmon. The story was rewritten for children in the 18th century and had become one of the most popular nursery stories by the Victorian period. Tiny characters resembling Tom also appear in folklore around the world.

The Magic Porridge Pot

The Magic Porridge Pot, also known as *Sweet Porridge*, is a German fairy tale, first recorded by the Brothers Grimm in 1825. The Grimms' version came from a storyteller called Dortchen Wild, who later became Wilhelm Grimm's wife. The set-up of the tale is similar to other European folk stories which features an out-of-control magical object. In a Norwegian tale called *Why the Sea is Salty*, the magic object is a salt mill that continues to turn out salt. Unable to stop it, the owner throws it into the ocean, which explains why the ocean is salty.

The Three Little Pigs

This story is one of the most popular fairy tales in Western culture. Printed versions of the tale date back to the 1840s, but the story is thought to be much older. It bears a strong resemblance to a tale collected by the Brothers Grimm in 1812, called *The Wolf and the Seven Little Kids*. This tale also features a "Big, Bad, Wolf," but he's hunting seven little goats rather than three little pigs. There are countless adaptations of the story. One of the best-known is Walt Disney's *Silly Symphonies* cartoon short created in 1933, which reimagined the tale for American audiences during the Great Depression.

The Little Red Hen

The Little Red Hen is an old folk tale, often believed to be of Russian origin. The earliest printed version of the tale appeared in 1874, and the simple celebration of work ethics and self reliance in the story made it an instant success. *The Little Red Hen* became a particularly popular nursery story in America in the 1940s, thanks to a series of children's books featuring the title character. Walt Disney's *Silly Symphonies* cartoon version from 1934 famously features the screen debut of Donald Duck.

Beauty and the Beast

Written and spoken versions of *Beauty and the Beast* have been around for centuries. An early telling of the story appeared in 1740, written by a woman called Madame Gabrielle de Villeneuve. Several years later, a French aristocrat called Madame Jeanne-Marie Le Prince de Beaumont adapted Madame de Villeneuve's tale for children, creating the version we know today. Since then, the story has had countless movie, book, television, and stage adaptations.

The Lion and the Mouse

The *Lion and the Mouse* is one of the best-known of Aesop's fables. The story has been reworked and expanded throughout the centuries, to touch on serious themes such as justice and politics, as well as being adapted into a popular children's tale, focusing on the importance of friendship. Versions of this tale exist in cultures around the world. In the Indian version, the lion becomes and elephant, and in China he is replaced by a tiger.

Town Mouse and Country Mouse

Town Mouse and Country Mouse is one of Aesop's fables. There have been various adaptations throughout the centuries. A Scottish version from the 1480s makes the mice sisters, while Jean de la Fontaine's French retelling of the tale features a country rat and a town rat. In 1918, the British author Beatrix Potter retold the story as *The Tale of Johnny Town-Mouse*. In this version, the country mouse falls asleep in a hamper and is carried away to the city where he meets Johnny Town-mouse, who later visits his friend in the countryside.

The Golden Goose

The Golden Goose is a fairy tale collected by the Brothers Grimm in the early 19th century. The Grimms' version of the tale follows the fortunes of the youngest brother after his discovery of the goose. The boy meets several characters who each try to take one of the bird's golden feathers and become stuck to the goose. The tale belongs to a tradition of stories about golden birds, such as Aesop's *The Goose That Laid the Golden Eggs*, *The Golden Mallard* in Buddist literature, and the "Huma bird" in Persian mythology.

The Enormous Turnip

The Enormous Turnip (also known as *The Giant Turnip*) is a fairy tale of Russian or Slavic origin. The tale was first published in a collection of children's stories in 1863, compiled by Russian publisher Alexander Afanasyev. Afanasyev published nearly 600 folk and fairy tales during his lifetime, and is often regarded as the Russian counterpart to the Brothers Grimm. There is a German tale called *The Turnip*, which appeared in *Grimms' Fairy Tales* in 1812, but it bears little resemblance to the Russian story.

The Hare and the Tortoise

This story is one of Aesop's fables. Although an original Greek version existed, there was no Latin translation of the story. As a result, unlike many of Aesop's other fables, the tale of *The Hare and the Tortoise* didn't appear in print until the 16th century. The first English language edition wasn't published until 1667. The tale belongs to a tradition of stories that focus on a race between unequal partners, which is usually won by some sort of trickery. There is a Native American tale, for example, in which Hummingbird and Crane decide to race from one ocean to another.

Sweet dreams…